Curse of a Lady Vampire

by

Jo Ann Atcheson Gray

Much Love !

DORRANCE
PUBLISHING CO
EST. 1920
PITTSBURGH, PENNSYLVANIA 15238

Dorrance Publishing Co
585 Alpha Drive
Pittsburgh, PA 15238
Visit our website at www.dorrancebookstore.com

ISBN: 978-1-6461-0480-2
eISBN: 978-1-6461-0721-6

Curse of a Lady Vampire

"Vampire de Dame"

"Lady Vampire"

The Beginning

 ʼm Annania. I want to tell you how I became a condemnation to myself as well as to my best friend, Sophia. This is a story to you of my life as it was and as it is now, or maybe let's just begin with the story of when my new life began. As I'm not sure the timing or the dates of all my experiences in this story; you must keep in mind I am immortal, and I've lived the undead life for many centuries now, so timing is something I cannot relate to. Too many centuries to remember the exact dates, but I will write what I can remember of my story. I will tell what I know as I think of it along the way. So, let's begin…

We lived in Alabama in the early 1800s on my parents plantation. The hills seemed to go on forever around it. Each one covered in the greenest grass you've ever seen. I remember so many childhood days spent wandering about pretending to be someone else, someone of importance. The pastures were full of beautiful horses, brooks, and streams that flowed for miles. The glorious, white plantation set on the highest hill. It seemed to tower over the workers' quarters, so they would always know who was in charge.

Long white columns followed the two-story home all the way up to the arched roof. The huge estate was sturdy yet flowing with its beautiful, tall beams running all the way up to what seemed like the sky. Banisters along the balconies circled the entire front of this lovely masterpiece. Each window seemed to be as stately as the trees where you could look out all around the residence to see the picturesque gardens and flowers along the entire grounds. Many rooms were filled with the most extravagant furniture money could buy. My family loved to show off their riches.

Sophia and I were both in our early twenties. We adored living here, but desired something more adventurous, mysterious. Oh wait! That's me! Sophia was always the content, easygoing one, but that wouldn't be for long.

It all started one stormy night with a knock at the front door. I think back hearing my father talking with a distinguished gentleman, dark, mysterious. A voice I'd never heard before, an exquisite French accent. It struck my inner darkness, fantasy. Sophia and I peered around the door of the sitting room to see a man seated at the desk with my father. He appeared to be a business man in his late thirties. I couldn't take my eyes off his tantalizing muscular body. Almost seeing through his refined attire, my mind kept teasing me about what was inside his pants. His hair was sinister black and reaching his broad shoulders, with eyes hollow, cold and occult. Exactly what I was yearning for!

My father spoke his name, calling him "Frederic," probing him about his journey from Paris. We giggled small laughs like little school girls. My father, hearing this, bid us to come in, but we speedily scooted up the stairs to our room.

After calming our giddiness, we rested across my bed.

Sophia warned, "You'd better leave him alone. He looks wickedly evil and out of your league. Besides he'll probably just break your heart like all the others."

"I don't care. I want him. Did you see those deep eyes? I could easily get lost in them."

She continued nagging, her voice fading. While I began fantasizing, gazing at my window thinking to myself, *I really want him...*

Interrupting my lustful thoughts, she said, "I wonder what he wants with your father? I'm sure it's business, of course, if only we knew what that business was."

"I wish it was me this mysterious man wanted. I wonder how long he'll stay...?" I questioned aloud.

Sophia replied, "You better get those thoughts from your mind. You know nothing of him."

Rolling my eyes at her, I faded back into my dream state, gazing out my window as the cruel rain fell steadily from the night sky.

It had been two weeks since I first saw Frederic, still not speaking a word to him. He never came out of the guest room upstairs during the daylight hours, and he always kept his door locked. He would only appear vaguely in the evening, and he'd leave on what he called a business meeting. I found myself occasionally daydreaming at his door on several occasions. He was extremely secretive, but I somehow loved it. Even though it ate at me to know his secret; he must have a secret. Otherwise, what does he do all day in that room of dead silence? Sophia seemed to careless, but I could see she, too, was just a little curious.

One early morning at sunrise, we were in the kitchen, finishing our breakfast at the bar.

"So, do you want to see why he keeps his door shut all day? Surely he's not in there, or he sleeps an awful lot," I said to Sophia as she took her last swallow of milk.

"We could get into a heap of trouble, Annania. What are you hoping to find? Can't you just leave well-enough alone?" Sophia pleaded.

"Well I'm going to see what I might find. Just can't stand it anymore. I have to know something about him."

Heading out the kitchen door, and up the staircase, Sophia followed as she mumbled, "You're crazy, but I'm right behind you as usual."

Smiling back at her as we approached his door, peeking through the keyhole, I saw no movement whatsoever. Tried to turn the knob, but of course, it was locked. Removing the skeleton key from my apron, I slipped it gently into the keyhole. Turning it quietly, opening the slightly creaking door, I slowly glanced my head around. No one was there. Sophia pushed at my back for me to go in.

Entering the room with her right at my heels, she whispered at me, "There's no one in here. I didn't see him leave out with your father this morning. Okay! So, you've seen his room, let's go! It's spooky in here."

"Ah! Quite spooky yet intriguing," I whispered back with a slight evil grin, saying, "Let's look around and see what we find, shall we?"

"Annania, you're just asking for trouble."

"Shut up, Sophia. Obviously, he's not in here so help me look through these desk drawers. Just stay quiet though, no one needs to know we are in here."

Shaking her head in disbelief but with no reply, she opened the first drawer. It was empty. She opened the rest only to find they were all empty as well. Looking around the room, we noticed his bed hadn't been touched.

"Does he sleep on the floor?" Sophia asked in bewilderment.

Not answering her I noticed a strangely large, black trunk underneath the window. Locked as well and without the right key, it frustrated me as we knelt beside it.

"I wonder what is in it... This is the same trunk I saw unloaded when he arrived. But why're his clothes stacked neatly in the corner? Why lock an empty trunk?" I asked in confusion.

Sophia just shook her head as if to say, "I don't know." Standing, we tried lifting it, but it was too terribly heavy; we couldn't even budge it.

"I've got to know what's in there!" I said, aggravated.

But we heard footsteps; someone was coming. Making haste, we slipped out of his room, closing the door leaning against it guiltily. We smiled innocently as the house maid passed by, nodding her head respectfully toward us. Deciding to try and open the trunk at another time, we speedily went back to the kitchen, acting as if we never left, placing the key back in the counter top drawer.

Of course, as days passed Frederic never spoke directly to us, he'd just pass by nodding his head politely tipping the rim of his hat. There was something in the way he looked at me when walking by. It was like his eyes were seeing straight through me to my very soul. It gave me shivers up my spine.

Then one evening just after dusk it happened. My life changed, never to be the same. It all started while Sophia and I were strolling arm in arm like two small girls through the rose garden behind our plantation, talking nonsense of Frederic's trunk and such. When he appeared suddenly right in our path, he spoke with a low seductive voice yet it was charming, polite. This was the first time he'd spoken to me.

Asking as he bowed, he spoke: "Would you mind walking with me on this lovely moonlit night, my lady?"

His French accent was so hypnotizing and intriguing, but I barely understood his English. Thinking this was exactly what I wanted to do, I said, "Yes sir. I'd love to accompany you."

Taking his arm, it felt cold as ice. I shivered slightly.

"Well, don't mind me. I'll just leave," Sophia snapped as she headed back toward the house, shaking her head but smiling.

While walking he spoke faintly of his home in Paris, his castle in Ireland, and other foreign soils he'd visited. His story amazed me whether it was true or not. It seemed I listened for hours, lost in the mere sound of his voice, as if I were a small helpless child.

Finally turning to me, he asked, all the while holding my hands in his, " Do you desire all I've spoken of and more, dear Annania? Do you desire me?"

Saying "yes" very cursorily, I found myself lost in his mystifying eyes, which were so spellbinding. Feeling a little frightened, I could sense they held a lot of secrets. Unable to move by his deep paralyzing stare, he took hold of me in his masculine arms kissing my lips so passionately. A kiss I had never experienced. Finally, I gave in to this kiss, instantly forgetting who or where I was. His lips were so cold, tasteless, yet warm and pleasurable at the same time, very strange and exciting.

Slowly, he caressed my face with his lips down my neck, still holding me tightly in his grip. Freely I gave in to his firm embrace. In one brief moment, my life changed as well as all that a vampire stood for. He bit my neck, even though making vampires of the female gender was forbidden. So naïve, yet still he bit me, draining me almost to my death. Feeling overwhelmed and oblivious, my thoughts and dreams filled his mind. I began to feel cold yet aroused, seemingly painless, like my soul was leaving my body, like dying, yet being reborn.

What is happening to me? I thought to myself. *Is this my death? What are you doing to me?*

Whispering softly to me, "You're a mistake I had to have. This is only the beginning, my love."

Giving himself to me the only way he could, instinctively as my body froze, I drank from his neck. As my teeth pierced his flesh, I could feel the warm blood on my tongue as I saw vaguely his thoughts, his dreams.

What was happening to me? My mind was racing as I fell limp.

He said seductively to me as he held me lifelessly in his embrace, "You're the first of your kind. You should know some rules about what you are becoming. You are now a curse. I'm in love with you already, Annania, and will keep you through eternity. I will return to you soon my love."

In an instant I was alone, helpless, and afraid. Dizzy and weak, I couldn't run nor scream. Falling to the ground, wanting to cry out, but I was seemingly paralyzed. I wasn't sure what to think or if I could think. Was this a dream? How could he leave me here alone? I felt like I was going far away now with time slipping away, not mattering. My memories flooded my mind, holding me to my past, my human nature. How could I leave this life in such a way as this? As my body began to grow colder, it seemed I was shaking uncontrollably without any rule over myself.

As fast as all this came, it stopped suddenly as I fell into a deep, mindless sleep. All was well, or so it seemed. Sweet bliss in this unknown. Tomorrow would be a new day, or would it? Was I dying? Had I left this world already? Was this what death felt like? Time was all I had now, or was it? Keep believing, that was all I could do. Would I live? Would I die? Was the night almost over? Would the sun rise soon? How long until I reached the end? Where would I go from here? I needed to decide now. Live or die? Just let go. I could feel it; my body was dying.

It was almost daylight when I awoke, my eyes opening sluggish. I ran to the house, entering as quietly as I could, making my way up the staircase to my room. Frightened, I wasn't quite sure what exactly was becoming of me. Was it all just a dream? Exhausted and weary, instinct was persuading me to hide from the sunlight barely coming through my window.

"But why? Could I be dead? A ghost?"

Sophia was sound asleep in bed across the room. Cautiously, I slid under my bed in a tight little corner, still afraid, and slept—not awakening until the following evening at dusk to find Sophia staring patiently at me in confusion.

Seeing plainly that she was wondering why I'd been under my bed all day, she asked me, "Why did you scream at me when I tried to wake you earlier? I could have sworn you growled a little."

Crawling out from under my bed, I looked at her; the aroma of her blood pumping through her body was almost unbearable. I could actually see the hint of blood coursing through her veins. It sent such a hunger pang throughout me, but I purposely fought it off, trying to ignore this mysterious sensation.

Looking extremely frightful to her, I'm sure, she reached out her hand as if to console me, but as her hand touched mine, she felt the rude coldness it exposed. Jumping back with slight fear, she saw that my skin was a pale white, almost like a ghostly figure. My eyes were dark and hollow; my teeth shown like a fiend with a touch of redness like bloodstains. Blood appeared to be stained on my neck and shoulder from last night's encounter.

When she turned to run, I promptly grabbed her by the forearm saying, "Don't be afraid of me, I'm okay! It's Frederic. He did this. He spoke of me being a curse of some kind now. Forbidden to be made into whatever I am. What that is, I'm not sure, but I'm guessing it's definitely not human. I'm sure I cannot be a ghost because you can feel me."

"You look terrible," Sophia stated as she swallowed hard, sitting down beside me. "Obviously you aren't dead, but you do look undead it seems."

Explaining further in detail to Sophia all that happened with Frederic, pausing in silence just slightly, I said, "I'm having this strange, unusual craving to taste blood. It's so strong like I've been starving for days. It frightens me somewhat."

"It sounds to me like you've become some kind of monster like in a horror story. You better be glad I love you, or I would bolt out of here. And it's a damn good thing your parents left early this morning. Well, if what you say is true, I'm sure we can find some blood... Perhaps from the smokehouse out back? Unbelievable, is what all this is. I told you to leave that man alone. I knew he was trouble. I could feel the evilness all over him!"

"No, Sophia, you don't understand. I want human blood. I want your blood. But I don't understand why.

No worries, I refuse to give in to temptation and bite you on what I think should be your neck vein."

"My blood! Human blood! With your teeth?! Are you crazy?! That's like murder! Like I said: Unbelievable!"

Rolling my eyes at her as she went on repeating the same questions, I glanced up at my nightstand between our beds and saw an envelope with my name written on it in French. Who knew I could read foreign language now? Picking it up, I translated the letter inside, which amazed me on how I could read it, it read as follows...

My Beloved Annania,

I'm so sorry to have made you what you are now. You are what is called a vampire. Yes, you are the myth you've heard about in stories. You'll be hungering for human blood by the time you read this, I'm positive. Please understand, I fell madly in love with you the very first time I saw you. I had to taste you, but something within me would not let me kill you, as I wanted to kill your parents. You changed my plans. You will be mine forever, my darling Annania.

You are to drink the blood of humans just as I did yours, but drink until they're dead; no more pulse. If they live, they will become as we are, and I do not recommend doing that. You'll find your peace, your joy, your solace in the warmth of the blood of your victims. I was fallacious for making you; it was forbidden. Still, I had to have you. The passion we shared between us was breathtaking! I will return to you soon, but until I do, you must know, there is a curse. I had forgotten it when I made you, maybe I didn't want to remember it at that moment. I'm so sorry, my love, but now I must live with my own guilt.

Please heed my warning, do not bite anyone else; especially females as to make them what you are now due to this curse being passed on to them. And most importantly, remember this always, stay out of the sunlight hours. It will destroy you. Only rise at dusk, rest in the day in a secure safe, dark place. Your body will become jade as the sun rises. You'll need to leave your beautiful home now, as you shall never die. I've enclosed two tickets to Paris. If you choose not to drink your friend's blood, take her with you, if you must, to be your keeper by day. I will contact you soon, my love. Always know, I love you, Annania. I will forever be watching you. Shall we live together through eternity. We are now sealed together by my blood, I warn you, never try to change that, my love.

Until I return to you, stay safe and happy hunting.

Frederic

Dropping the letter to floor, I sat down slowly on my bed, speechless. Sophia seated herself next to me, putting her arm across my shoulders. I realized then I could read her thoughts. She was actually fearful of me, yet calm. I could see she was truly worried about me.

"Well, that explains what had possibly been in his trunk," I mumbled to myself, slightly grinning.

Over the next few nights, we were prepared for our trip to Paris. A carriage was ready out front where we were to go to the vessel that would take us on our journey. We carried a large, over-sized trunk with us in which I would sleep by day while Sophia watched over me.

On the ship, I generally lingered in my cabin most nights, except for the killing of insects and small rodents on deck while no one was about. I could see others were whispering among themselves about us, two women, all alone on such an immense voyage. But they never attempted to hinder us. I was hungering for blood so viciously inside myself but was terrified to kill someone. I tried satisfying this thirst by killing rodents of various sizes as I mentioned earlier. It worked for only a short while, never seeming to satisfy my inner desire. Sophia kept repeating to me how grouchy and moody I was becoming. I have to admit, I was miserable, weak, and unbearable at times. She luckily stayed right with me the entire ocean trip, never giving up on me. But I noticed she would get aggravated at me a few times.

Arriving in Paris, we arranged for a flat above a diminutive coffee shop. The room was slender, but we had no complaints. We relaxed our first night there, not going about any place. Sophia was all snuggled in her wool blanket, reading her favorite book she read since she was in her teens. Feelings would arise as I would gaze at her, thinking I could lose her. It was an atrocious feeling.

We were there for several days when I succumbed to my thirst.

"Sophia, I've got to have something other than this market blood. I want real blood, warm and substantial. I can't stand it any longer, this pathetic torment."

"You mean, you would actually take someone's life? Drain their body completely of their disposition? You can't be serious… But I believe you are. I see it in your eyes. Almost scary, those eyes of yours."

As she spoke these words to me, her blood was pulsing through her veins as if her skin was pure glass, porcelain. It maddened me. I was all but tasting it. Noticing the evil glare on my face as I watched her she asked me in a shaky alarming voice, "Annania, are you okay?"

No answer.

"Are you okay?" she asked again, much bolder this time.

Finding my wits, I shook the thoughts from my mind as vastly as they came and said in a sickened state as left the room, "I'm going out alone tonight for a while, Sophia. I'll be back soon. Don't wait up for me. Believe me, this is for your own safety."

I left her there, speechless. She knew what I was about to accomplish, but at this point, there was no stopping me. No guilt. I had to have some human blood before I go mad.

Walking the dirty, sinister streets of Paris as a seemingly crazed lunatic, I saw a peddler standing alone with his hand out as if to receive a free meal from the passersby. Watching him like a lion would its prey, I finally walked straight up to him and gripped his throat, moving so swiftly even I was amazed. I carried him into the darkened alley down the street, hurling so fast that the human eye couldn't see. He never knew what had him as I sank my fangs deep into his venous blood vessel. The blood was so warm, so inviting as it streamed down my throat. Seeing his fears, his sins, his lustful thoughts of the past until they vanished. His heart ceased to beat. The deed was done. I took my first life. I dropped his lifeless body to the cold dark gray street, drained to his death. I had taken a life.

Afterwards, I walked for what seemed for hours, taking it all in. Feeling indestructible yet ugly. A life was taken by my sinful lust of wanting to satisfy my own desires. Guilt set in as I got closer to my flat. I felt such guilt, not for murdering this wretched human, but mostly for killing him to fill my own blood lust. I've become a fiend and will be one for all existence. Guilt for feeling so amazing and completely satisfied. I was at peace within myself. So, this is who I am now.

After this night, it all seemed to get easier. Even the guiltiness was forgotten as long as I could taste the blood. Ah! The warm blood! So fulfilling! Giving me peace, joy, just as Frederic said it would. Sophia had been right; I had become a monster.

Over the next few nights, Sophia and I shopped in the little boutiques and did practically everything together, except for the nights I would drink from some despicable person. I just didn't think Sophia could handle seeing the sight of such actions. She, at this point, hasn't mentioned it or brought it up. Maybe she's cautious to ask about the details.

Although, I started having intense sensitivity for her, wanting her to experience the awesomeness I felt when I would drain a human being of their blood. The feeling of being fierce and audacious, like I could conquer the world. On the face of it, I was on an astonishing selfish power trip. Yes, she saw the difference in my character, my actions, my personality, yet she never spoke of it.

One late evening, I returned early from drinking blood to find Sophia had been crying. Standing at the window as I entered the doorway, she said to me, "It's your parents. They were found dead days ago. Our home was burned completely. They think it was someone who possibly robbed them and set the house aflame afterwards. It's all on this telegram from your Aunt Helen, who also says not to come. The funeral would be over by the time we arrived. Apparently, the land and the assets left there belongs to you now. The land deeds and inheritance are being sent to us."

I was taken aback as I took the telegram from her hand, sitting on my bed she sat beside me as I started to cry for the first time since my change. Tears of blood smudged my face as I stopped myself wiping my hand over my eyes and said potently, "Well, it's over. It's done. No need to weep forever. Forever is all I got. Looks like I better get used to moments of sadness like this."

Sophia just cried quietly to herself as I relaxed myself on my bed, thinking to myself. Sure, I was saddened greatly by the news of their deaths, but we were never a real close family anyway. Besides, it's hard to feel too much when your heart doesn't have much spirit left in it. The only person I have ever really been remotely close to would be Sophia. I don't want to ever lose her. Oh, my dear Sophia! She's closer than what a sister or a friend would be. She's been with me since her parents were killed in an accident when she was only 10 years old. Not sure how it happened, but as an only child, it was wonderful to have someone. Tears were starting to swell up in my eyes again as it dawned on me that Sophia will die one day. Selfishly, I wanted her to stay with me and be mine forever. I couldn't stand the thought of her gone.

Looking at her, I moved closer, hugging her. She had stopped crying by now and was just sitting in silence. Her thick, long, blonde hair was a beautiful mess hanging over her shoulders. In my eyes, she was such a fragile thing, so beautiful, so picturesque. Of course, I'm not bad looking either. My black hair was longer than hers, a little past my waist. There I go, being vain again.

Anyway, back to the story…

"Sophia, do you want to be together everlastingly, never dying?"

"That would be marvelous, I think, to never die, but how could I possibly do what you do to people?"

"Oh, it comes easy enough in time, I promise."

Of course, I was lying. It eats at you every night, except when drinking the blood.

"Do you trust me?" I pleaded to her.

"How do you know it will even work? What if you mess up and kill me?" Sophia questioned eagerly.

"I'll do it just as Frederic did it to me. I remember what he did. Then we will see what happens. You gotta trust me," I stated boldly yet sweetly.

Nodding her head, she whispered, "Yes, but is it going to hurt?"

"Not for long, you'll see," I whispered back, comforting her as I leaned in to her neck, kissing the place

I intended to bite. Gently, I sank my teeth into her warm, soft, pink flesh. Screaming out in a painful sensation, she never once moved away. I consumed her blood until I could see her thoughts, fears, and dreams so vividly. Instinct was telling me to stop, but I was in too deep to just pull away. This blood was holding me to her. Screaming my name, she pushed against me to cease. I thought to myself, *I must halt or she'll die,* but the blood was overpowering my senses. Then suddenly without reason, I came to my consciousness, pulling myself from her. Shaking fiercely as her body started to grow colder. In an instant, she jumped from the bed falling over into the floor circling around like she was possessed with something. As she turned onto her back, I slipped in beside, her placing my neck on her lips giving myself to her. Greedily, she drank from me. Never had I perceived so much rage, so much anger, power from her. Sophia was changing into something far better than what I could imagine. My gentle fragile Sophia would be no longer.

Pushing her away, she began to laugh uncontrollably. Was this my sweet Sophia? Calming down slowly, she finally passed out, sleeping for several hours it seemed. I stayed by her side; it felt like an eternity until she awoke. Cold and pale as I was, she was even more beautiful in my eyes than she had been before. Upon awakening, she looked straight at me saying, "I'm hungry for blood."

Thrilled to hear these words coming from her satin burgundy lips, I took her hand, leaving out the door to the dreadful streets of Paris. Funny thing, who knew she'd be more of a heartless killer than I was? All I could think of was how proud I was and what exactly did I just create. Thoughts ended when we spotted an elderly couple sitting snugly on a corner bench. We swiftly approached them taking them into the dark night sinking our teeth deep in their wrinkled flesh. I had the old man; Sophia chose the little old lady. Who would've guessed she would catch on so fast? She actually killed better her first try than I did. Finishing this old man off before she was done, I just sat on the ground watching her as that little old lady went limp. Seemed she already to know what to do. Sophia dropped her to the dampened street, peering up at me and said, "I feel I could conquer the world. This blood is so fulfilling!"

"Believe me, I know how satisfying it can be. Don't fret over them. They were useless anyway," I said with a wicked grin.

Devilishly, Sophia replied, "Don't worry, I wasn't going to fret."

Making haste as to return to our room before sunrise, we talked and laughed awhile about the nights events as we proceeded to curl up together in my large trunk.

As we snuggled closely, Sophia said, "Annania, I really enjoyed tasting that old lady tonight. Guess this is where guilt is haunting me. Was I wrong? Why the sudden guilt, yet I loved it?"

"I don't know those answers, Sophia, but this has to be our eternal damnation somehow. We are, maybe, monsters now, possibly damned to hell. Oh well, at least we'll stay together forever. Now go to sleep, my everlasting blood companion."

As we slept so intimately in each others arms, like a mother embracing her child, I completely failed to remember this little bite from me to her would release me of the curse, passing it on to her.

Drifting into a wakeless, sound sleep… I could see myself as a young toddler, safely in my mother's arms back at my plantation. Mother, rocking me ever so gently, sang an old gospel hymn to me in front of the warm burning fireplace. As I started to cry, she softly sat me on the small sofa.

I was trying to tell her that Sophia was hurt, but she wouldn't listen. I could hear Sophia in my mind, as I sat just crying, pleading to my mother. Mentally, Sophia was screaming at me not to kill her. But why me??

Then in an instant, this nightmare changed. Sophia and I were much older and in some strange, dark park. It was dreary and raining intemperately. These wicked creatures were flying above the dispiriting oak trees that surrounded us. Circling us like human-sized bats, they kept swooping down at us trying to consume us. We screamed and pleaded for someone, anyone, to help; one of these dreadful beings suddenly picked Sophia up, carrying her away. Trying my best to catch her, it just flew higher and higher, shouting back to me as I stood there helpless and crying, almost like an echo.

"Sophia, will die. It's all your fault."

At this point, it let her go. She was falling; no matter how I tried, I couldn't catch her. Right before her seemingly lifeless body approached the ground, I awoke.

Sophia had already awakened, standing beside the window and was gazing at the street below with another letter in her hand.

I asked as I walked over to her, "Who's the letter from this time?"

"Read it yourself," she said harshly, tossing the letter toward me somewhat angrily.

Opening it, I found it was from Frederic.

"But how would he know where we were staying?" I asked aloud, a little confused, looking up at her.

"Just read it. It explains everything," Sophia snapped as she pushed pass me, bumping my shoulder.

Quietly, I began reading it as I seated myself beside her on the edge of the bed…

My Beloved Annania,

I just knew you'd pass the curse on to your friend. I also remind you that I'm always watch-

ing you. Please understand the curse is now on your friend. She must now begin her quest for a mortal male to conceive a girl child by and very soon. He must be willing to partake in the intercourse. Know this, time passes much quicker for us vampires. So, make haste and find your dear acquaintance a mate.

When this female child is born, she must choose on her seventeenth birthday to become a vampire or stay as a mortal. It must be done by the first full moon of that year. If by chance she does accept her fate as a vampire, the curse will then pass onto her, and the whole process repeats itself. Wouldn't it be marvelous to populate the entire world with our kind?! Leaving mortals only to be our slaves! Only a mere joke, my love.

Otherwise, if she chooses to live a mortal life the curse will end, and so shall us all. It will destroy you, Annania, and all that we are. Your lovely friend shall know the right man when she sees him, like an attraction that can't be ignored. Heed my warning; absolutely no male child is to be formed. He will become a monster and will have to be killed immediately after birth. This needs to work especially to my advantage, so please cooperate, and do exactly as I've instructed you.

Be aware of the one they call "the Man," who seeks to destroy you as well as us all. Stay on alert

*of him; he's extremely dangerous. Be cautious of
everyone at this crucial time. I love you, Annania. Always trust in me. You are mine now forever. Never forget that. I will return to you soon,
my love.*

*Oh, and I'm dreadfully sorry for the loss of
your family. It saddens my entire being to hear
such news. Until I see you again, much love!*

Frederic

Sitting there speechless, I thought to myself, *Could
all this actually be true?* I had done this to Sophia. She
now has to complete my fate. It was supposed to be me
who endured this wretched curse, not her.

Seeing she was still tempestuous, I wondered if she
blamed me. Of course, she had to. I was a terrible fiend
to have put this on her. How did Frederic possibly
know of my parents' mishap? It made me curious as to
where he was now. Lord, what have I gotten us mixed
up in? And for love or lust, I did this to us.

Interrupting my thoughts, Sophia spoke, "I made
my own decision, Annania. No, I'm upset but not really
at you. I'm frustrated at the whole situation. Frederic
could have explained this to you, making it clear before
he turned you, but he didn't. I don't blame you. I blame
him. What's done cannot be undone."

"I'm sorry, Sophia, for what I've set upon you."

Leaning over as to hug me, she whispered, "At least we'll always be together. Now let's go out and start looking for that mate."

Asking out of pure curiosity as we left the room, "But why don't you just pass this curse over to some stranger, some mixed-up woman on drugs or something? Just bite one. Then the curse is lifted from yourself and not on our conscience any longer? And stop reading my thoughts, it's just weird."

"That's just not in me, Annania, to pass this condemnation on, and besides, I'd rather leave our immortal fates up to us, not some stranger. It would only make for more confusion, I believe. You quit reading my mind because I know you do it very often. I'm curious about what Frederic said in that letter. Is he being serious about populating the world? Seems creepy, don't ya think?"

Not answering, I suggested, "Let's have a blood feast instead," pointing in the direction of two skinny punk teenage lovebirds on the street ahead of us.

Moving in teasingly with boy, Sophia and I playfully started to caress him, as the young girl joined in with what seemed to be raging hormones. Their drunken thoughts were of a dirty seductive nature, with visions of a foursome. So sad, it would never make it that far…

Sinking my fangs deep into his neck, he screamed out in pain, trying to run but to no avail. The girl tried to fight her way loose from Sophia, but no such luck.

All she could do was scream and cry for help as she watched her lover being sucked dry of his life. Dropping his lifeless body to the cobblestone street, I looked up at the girl with an evil, bloody grin on my face. Yes, she was horribly afraid; I didn't care. Winking at Sophia, she turned this being in her arms around, swiftly sinking her teeth into her vein. This spirited girl screamed louder putting up a courageous fight with Sophia, but she began to grow weaker and weaker as Sophia drained her. She was no more.

Lifting both bodies, we carried them to the closest darkest alley we could find and dropped them. Rather quickly, I must add, no human eye could have noticed.

"It sure was a good thing there weren't any passersby," I said jokingly as Sophia and I merely strolled down the street like nothing ever happened.

"What do you say to a play tonight down at the picturesque theater?" Sophia roguishly suggested.

"That would be wonderfully relaxing. I need a good laugh anyways."

When we returned home, we curled up so tightly together in our compartment and slept.

My dreams returned to me. This time, Sophia was crying, running down a long, dark, mysterious road. She was only an infant child, yet I was much older and trying to catch her, but I couldn't run quite fast enough. The scenario went over and over in my mind until finally, at that moment, I saw Frederic. He was standing with his arms outstretched at the end of the darkened path. There were several scars on his face, which stood out to me in the darkness.

Picking Sophia up in his masculine arms as she approached the end of this road, he shockingly broke her tiny fragile neck. He looked up at me with such evil in his sunken eyes while he held her lifeless body.

Screaming in anguish at him, I pleaded, "I'll kill you for that! How could you? I thought you loved me!"

He began laughing uncontrollably at me as I was running it seemed like an eternity to get to where he stood. The more I ran, the further away he became. His laugh was becoming an echo in my mind as he slowly turned and walked away with her defenseless body, dead, limp, in his arms. As they disappeared into the vast darkness, I awoke, breathing heavily with blood sweat dripping from my face. Sophia was still sluggishly lying next to me.

This dream reoccurred, playing over again and again in my slumbers for several nights... Why? I was not exactly clear as to its meaning. Maybe it was because of the love I had for these two, or perhaps it was fear of losing my Sophia. In any case, I knew it was part of the curse that was upon me, eternal torment through my dreams. It had to be my punishment for this evil creature I've become.

One thing comes to mind, I can't distinguish if this was a vision, a dream, or an actual sighting. In a cloudy haze, I could see my mother in all her beauty wearing a white gown of satin. In my mind, I was thinking she was probably buried in this. Her long, flowing salt and pepper hair was blowing in the misty breeze as she appeared to be reaching her arms out to me in a consoling manner. She was saying, ever so silently, that she loved me still, even though I was a monster now. She was telling me she would continue to pray for my soul, no matter the circumstances. Then she slowly faded away in the mist as quickly as she appeared. Silence. I continued to gaze out my window, not sure why I saw my mother that night. I wasn't afraid, but it did shiver me up just a little. Deep down, I did miss her. I never saw her again. I remember pondering on how Sophia and I lived back then. So simple, it seemed. So much has changed now.

Some time has passed by now. Sophia and I are still residing in Paris after traveling around the world together, seeing things we loved and some things we hope to forget.

One place comes vividly back to my memory. It was in Ireland, not sure the exact location now. Spending our time there mostly in a little local pub, joking about the bartender, we remotely sat at the bar, talking about his tight jeans and how good he would taste. But his margaritas seemed to be too good to everyone, so we decided to let him live to make a few more. That same night as we sat patiently waiting at the bar, I decided I was in the mood for someone a little more vicious. Searching and watching what seemed like hours, we finally found victim. Reading his thoughts, he kept his wife at home with a stern hand while out with mistresses of the evening.

"Yes, he will do nicely, Sophia. I found dinner. You can bring the wine."

Smiling mischievously as she read my thoughts, she mindfully replied, "I hope he left his better half something large in his will."

"But of course," I thought back, "we can't forget the ladies of the night."

Both harlots, not knowing about the spouse waiting at home worrying about her husband.

Half past midnight, we followed the drunken trio out into the shadows of the night as they walked the dusty streets back to his lair, obvious for playful intentions. It's such a shame they would never reach this destination.

As we slowly approached them, I commented aloud, "Sophia, I just love this part of the game. It's always easier when they're confused, afraid, not understanding what's about to happen, poor wretched creatures they are."

She giggled a slight chuckle as she moved closer to them, asking, "Would you guys like some extra company for the evening?"

Shocked slightly in his drunken condition, the man smiled curiously, nodding his head lustfully in reply.

Luring them closer to us, playfully, I was patiently waiting for the fun to begin. Noticing all the passersby were out of sight, there was silence except for our party's giggles. Sophia, rather close to one of the ladies, began sharing a kiss. In one sudden moment, the bliss began. Gripping her tightly, Sophia began feeding on her main artery. Yelling in fear like a mouse running from the cat, the man started to run, but I appeared swiftly, ghostly, turning him around in one jolt, grasping his bare rugged neck as I joined Sophia in our perfect feast. All the while, the other lady of pleasure ran away, screaming for help. Something new to report in the news, I suppose. Another myth about vampires to be told.

Ah, that was such an exciting time in our travels!

Our estate in Paris is extraordinary. By day, it's watched over by paid servants and a well-respected lawyer named Francis. We call her Frankie. She handles all our business affairs and personal finances, as well as she's the one who runs the estate. Living within our walls, she also handles our staff daily, protecting our privacy nightly. Not knowing exactly what we might be, she respects the pretty dollar amount. Thinking we work quietly in our chambers all day on business matters, she knows never to disturb us for any reason. Of course, we keep ourselves locked in tight in our dwellings with no one having a key.

I'm sure she is suspicious as to who we are, but she never questions us. She only does her job as instructed.

A very loyal, tactful friend and worker, so long as she has control over the estate with a nice payroll.

Almost like a castle, our entire property is very large. You can only imagine how beautiful this Victorian style mansion could be with its lovely flowered yard and extravagant rose garden that surrounds the spacious grounds. We love it here!

Years it seems that we aged, but we never show any signs of it. Sophia still hasn't developed the urge to pursue a man. We just been enjoying life or the lack thereof. We've met and devoured many a male but with no luck as to find her mortal.

One evening strolling into the sitting room, Sophia handed me the weekly paper with a devilish grin across her lips.

"Look, you're famous now."

The paper dated March 25, and on the front page was an article of a serial killer with a vampire style running loose on the nighttime streets of Paris.

"Well, you know, I'm not working alone," I replied with a sarcastic tone.

"Yes, I know. You've made it so you'll never be alone," snapped Sophia slavishly.

"You're just distressed cause you haven't found a man in the last century!"

We both laughed.

Getting back to our travels, it seems we have been everywhere and seen so many things, and met so many different people, some good, some bad, some we eat, some we graciously let live. We've visited many places, plus we have recent t-shirts to prove it.

Along the way, we encountered a few male vampires, and feeling they despised us, we never actually made contact or communicated with any them. But I'm almost positive they accept us by now.

One rainy, stormy night comes to mind... It was while we were visiting Italy, we'd had a tiresome night of feasting. Wet and sluggish, Sophia and I were on our way back to our suite when along the cobblestone path we had our first sighting of the opposite sex of our kind.

"Do you feel their eyes?" I whispered fearfully as I tried to sense in the darkness where they might lurk.

"What do you suppose they want?" Sophia whispered back.

"Maybe they're as curious about us as we are of them. But who cares," I said. "We need to go now. The sun will be rising soon."

Hastily, we scurried along, leaving them behind in the shadows with their curiosities to worry about another night. Honestly, I just wasn't up for the fight if there would've been one. I'm sure they wondered about us being female and immortal. Exactly what they were feeling, I guess it forever be a mystery.

We had a few more convergences, but none as creepy as that particular night.

Yes, "the Man" has chased us from time to time along our way, but he never gets so close as to harm us. We've never actually seen him, only sensed his presence.

Frederic joined us in while passing through Venice, where we stayed for a few days. So thrilled to see him, I'm afraid I neglected Sophia somewhat. He and I shared those evenings with an intense dose of passion, barely feeding, except on each other.

She gave us our privacy, staying away most of the time. I kind of missed her, but only slightly, as I was occupied... I believe she went about from man to man during our stay here, trying to find the right male but with no success.

Finally, the three of us returned together to Paris. To this day, I still haven't a clue as to Frederic's dwelling and where it's located in Europe. I've only visited on occasion his luxurious castle in Ireland. Beautiful and set apart from any civilization. But that's to be told later.

My dear Frederic comes and goes as he well pleases. And yes, he does please! Oh sorry, back to my story...

We stay in contact, or should I say when he decides to grace me with his presence. He always pleads for me to leave with him but without Sophia. But how could I ever leave her? She's so fragile to me. She needs me, and I, her. A connection I cannot explain, like a union that can never be split apart.

Back to our return to Paris...

During Sophia and I's travels and experiences, we had our enormous mansion built, along with the land developed. Money was no option. As vampires it comes our way easy enough. We will just leave that bit of information to one's own imagination. Once we returned from our journeys to Paris with Frederic at my side, we laid eyes on our beautiful, overwhelming home. It was breathtaking!

Sophia took an interest in music, practicing the piano and guitar. She began buying and selling them both over the internet, as they call it, with Frankie handling all aspects of it.

I took to writing novels with various artist's names who do not really exist. Writing became my passion, as long as I wasn't drinking blood of my victims. Throughout my travels, I would write or some would say scribble stories here and there about something that inspired me at that precise moment. After returning home, I began to turn them into novels and stories. Frankie helped get my novels published, and it began from there. I'm sure you've probably read my books and do not realize it, as I cannot reveal the names I write under.

Sophia and I really enjoyed our travels and our days of peacefulness at home. My horrid dreams have even ceased for a while, but they'll return soon. Everything seemed to be going well for us, like living the high life. Having seen everything we ever dreamed of, yet we would forget that we were still vicious monsters of the darkness and that a curse was still upon us. Our lives as we know it were about to take a twist.

One evening in the city district of Paris, Sophia and I decided to go shopping and throw our wealth around. Strolling along the busy sidewalks, looking at the window displays, is when it finally happened. Sophia spotted a man across the way from us. Noticing he was quite appealing to her, I got the impression right away she wasn't going to kill this one.

Making her way leisurely over to him she seductively said, "Hello."

It all started from that point on. "True Love."

Of course, he was handsome, but it sickened me. I just went into the store of the window display I was standing next to.

Learning later after her arrival home that his name was Victor, she explained that he was in his late forties, lives in America, and is known as what they call a "drug lord" in today's language. This relationship grew and went on for a long while. They would date as much as they could while he was in town. Becoming close friends and somewhat intimate, Sophia wanted him to be the male she would choose. She even admitted to actually loving him.

I asked her one night as we sat in our study, "How can you love a guy you only see once every three months? You know you can't keep him. You're a fiend, and he's human."

Responding quick and slightly harsh, she said, "How can you love a vampire who you only see once or twice every six months? Besides you know nothing of Frederic's past."

"You know it's different between him and I. We've known each other a hell of a lot longer. In any case, we are both vampires, monsters, joined together by blood. You already know this. Please, just do not get to attached to this mortal. That's all I'm saying."

"I don't care," Sophia snarled. "I still want him. All I have to do is keep him long enough to get pregnant with a girl child."

"What about his drug career?" I asked teasingly.

"I couldn't care less about that. After all, I murder on a daily basis most of the time. Do I not?"

Laughing, breaking the tension, we went to our bedroom and climbed in our coffin. Yes, we still share our eternal resting place. Always will, if I have a say in it.

As I slumbered, my first dream in ages began... I could see Victor and Sophia. They were upset and arguing. I'd been angry toward them for some strange reasoning. Turning, she looked at me as she held a small baby boy swaddled in a thin blanket. Walking over to her rather quickly I noticed as I approached that this baby boy was horrifying. A noticeable amount of blood was dripping from its head where it appeared Sophia had bitten him. This thing was crying out very loudly. Panicked, I screamed out, "This is a monster! We have to kill it!"

Victor shouted defensively in response as he stood close to Sophia "No! He's my son! You're the monsters, you should die!"

Coming at me suddenly with a knife, he stabbed me in the temple of my skull. Bleeding fiercely, I could see Sophia, all the while, was shouting at me, "It's all your fault! It's all your fault, Annania!"

It started to deafen me as the sound of her voice faded like an echo. Then I awoke, shaking, breathing intemperately as the evening was forthcoming.

Sophia had a date scheduled with Victor this night, so she had already awakened and left. She was supposed to meet him at the little café down the street, their favorite spot of late.

Staying in, I awaited the long-anticipated arrival of my Frederic.

Victor and Sophia were having dinner, or least he was eating, and they were talking about future plans to be made when his cell phone began to ring. Jumping to his feet as he answered it, he toppled his chair over, suddenly slamming his phone shut. Placing it back into his pocket, he clutched Sophia's wrist.

"We've got to go. Hurry, come with me! There's something I've got to handle. Wow, your hand is still freezing!" he stated hastily.

As they came upon an old abandoned warehouse a few blocks from the little café, it was very damp and wet inside. She could sense there was trouble. Before she could speak a word, a loud, deafening gun shot fired from across the room. The bullet came straight for Victor, hitting him in his face sailing him backward to the floor. Instinctively, she dashed for the human holding the rifle. She speedily pulled the weapon from his hands, sinking her fangs deep into his neck draining him completely of the blood that flowed within him. He never knew what took him. The other men around him ran away in fear, dropping their guns to the floor as scurried out the entrance of the warehouse.

Returning to Victor, Sophia could see he was already deceased. Kneeling beside him, she began kissing his blood stained lips pleading loudly, "Why did this have to happen? I wanted him!"

Gently laying his lifeless body back to floor, she stood up, angered, blood tears in her eyes, feeling broken, she concluded it had to be something to do with a bad drug deal.

Of course, she killed, devoured many humans that night, feeling revengeful like a heartless demon. Yes, a few days after, it was all in the paper about a deranged serial killer still on the loose.

Meanwhile, that same night at home, Frederic and I were having a lovely romantic evening together. He had arrived at my door moments after awakening. As I greeted him, he swiftly scooped me up in his masculine arms kissing and caressing me ever so slowly. Falling onto the bed as we were embraced tightly together, he began telling me how much he had missed touching and holding me.

Almost in a faint whisper, I told him, "I love you."

Gazing into each other's eyes, I could smell his enchanting blood pulsing through his veins. Knowing completely that he was doing the same and really yearning to taste him, he leaned into me, kissing my lips down to my neck while whispering, "I want you."

Shifting my neck as to invite him, he sank his teeth into my vein, drinking covetously from me. It pained me, yet I loved it. It was a pleasurable, torturous feeling of lust that surrounded my entire body. When finished, he looked up at me as blood drizzled from his stained lips. He started kissing me again as I tasted the warm blood on his lips. Engrossing firmly, I cupped his jaw in my hands as he pulled me closer to him wrapping his arms around my waist.

Placing me on his domain, I began foreplay down his neck sinking my teeth into his flesh. Warm and so fulfilling was his blood. He let me drink my fill until it was just overwhelming. Gazing back into his eyes, we kissed again, deep yet slow, falling in place as we embraced on the bed. As we lay there completely satisfied and relaxed, we talked about petty things for what seemed like hours. He told me stories of his recent travels, and I spoke of Sophia and how we had been doing. He secretly pleaded at times for me to just leave with him, never to look back. But he already knew I could never leave my sweet Sophia. So closely we were embraced, we felt completely lost to the world around us. Staying this way for a while, we only kissed, talked, and shared our blood along with a few mindful, yet lustful desires.

Now that I've told you what Frederic and I were doing, let's get back to Sophia...

After murderously taking several mortal lives, she arrived home still discomposed, slightly winded as she ran up the spiral staircase to my bedroom door. Frederic and I were still dwelling comfortably across my bed as she rushed over placing herself at our feet. Immediately, I could see something was wrong with her. She was covered in blood of her victims. She poured her soul out to us of all that happened this night. Too much sadness, Frederic took his exit bidding us both farewell. Consoling her as best, I could we slowly strolled over to our coffin and settled in, sleeping so entwined I could actually feel her pain. Who knew as vampires we could feel so much without a heartbeat? Slipping into sweet slumber, we were as one.

You guessed it; my dreams haunted me... I had a horrible dream of Victor and Sophia. He was laying on the cold, dampened street while she held him tightly to her breasts, crying profusely and cursing at me. He was slowly dying in her arms. Blood was scattered all around them. She kept cursing me and chanting these words at me... "It's all your fault!" It maddened me in my sleep. Her words repeated over and over, getting louder as she screamed them.

Then I awoke, angered within myself, thinking, *Why must I keep having these nightmares? Shall they remain for all eternity?*

Calming myself as I lay quietly beside Sophia, I decided to wake her up. Luckily it was already dusk.

We feasted then went to dwell in the local park as we sat on a cold yet cozy bench. Watching people as they passed us by, we overheard two old elderly ladies who appeared to be in their late seventies. They spoke of their past experiences within their lifetime. They discussed their aches and pains they now suffer with. One out talking the other. Dressed in stiletto heels, fake costume jewelry galore, and enough makeup to make a clown blush, they continued on about their families, or whoever wouldn't come to visit them, as they seated themselves across the way from us on the little wooden bench. They went on and on about their loved ones who had gone on before them into their great eternity above.

Playfully, I hinted to Sophia, "You know that will never happen to you and I. Let's end their misery, shall we?"

Never blinking, Sophia closed in on them so fast, I almost laughed out loud. I followed her move. Poor wretched ladies didn't even know what took them. They weren't even able to take in a deep breath.

Leaving their miserable, wrinkled bodies behind as if we were never even there, all was silent as we made our way back to our estate. We felt a hint of guilt between us, trying to justify ourselves by agreeing those two little old beings were soon to die anyways.

A few nights passed by, and we attended the funeral viewing of Victor, which his nearest relative held for him in Paris. It was a large turn out of his family, or what I thought to be his family. No one knew who we were, and we didn't recognize any of them. Only reading some of their thoughts from time to time, we didn't stay too awfully long; just long enough for Sophia to say her goodbyes. On our way out of the enclosure, she noticed a man standing alone outside the funeral parlor. After reading his mind, apparently this person was Victor's younger brother. Stubbornly, Sophia decided it to be the best thing to choose him to be her mate.

We stood across the street from him several minutes, just watching him. Sophia contemplated on how she would introduce herself. We gathered from his mind's ramblings that he was an outcast to his family, divorced, and very unhappy about the curves life had thrown him. He appeared much younger in appearance than Victor yet favored him tremendously. As his thoughts raced on, we discovered that Victor was the family's pick of the litter. Only his brother knew of his secret lifestyle. This brother was deemed as the "black sheep," but Victor was his only family member to truly care for him.

Breaking the silence, I spoke impatiently, "Are we going to stand here all night? Or are you going to go over and speak to this miserable being?"

She just rolled her eyes at me as she finally went toward him. She shook his hand and began talking with him. Seemingly, they were hitting it off quite nicely. After hearing what his name was, which was Anthony, I lost interest. Scanning the brains of the small crowd that accumulated out front of the parlor, you wouldn't believe the stuff in other people's minds. The way they think, and how they judge one another!

Casually, with a hint of a flirtatious walk, Sophia came back over to where I was abiding and stated, "Yes, he will do just fine. I want him. The funny thing is, he didn't even ask how I knew Victor. He seemed to just enjoy the companionship and the fact he's getting to have a conversation. Poor lonely creature."

"Can we leave now? These mortal's thoughts are exhausting! If I stay any longer, I might snap, or actually start feeling sorry for these piteous multitudes. These people are starting to freak me out a little. Sophia, you wouldn't believe the things these people have in their heads! And they call us devils."

Anxiously, we got back to our cozy sleeping quarters, not really in the mood to feed tonight. We went over the night's happenings and about this Anthony. Curiously, I asked her, "Are you sure you're not just wanting this guy because of your feelings for Victor?"

"I know he's definitely the one. I can't explain it," she snapped. "Now go to sleep. I'm tired."

As the nights passed on, Sophia frequently met with Anthony on many occasions. They would laugh and talk like school kids falling in "puppy love." They seemed to be getting closer and closer to each other. It made me sick to my stomach at times, quite silly and pathetic. It looked as if two broken hearts were consoling one another. Besides, he came across to me as a wimp of a man, unlike his brother Victor. At least Sophia was ostensibly happy for now.

Yes, he was going to be the one who would help Sophia have her girl child. Wasn't he in for a grand surprise! I couldn't wait to see the look on his face when it's over and done. As you can damn well determine, I really disliked him! I'd be pleased when we could just kill him! She has to stop getting so attached to this being!

During Sophia's courtship I occupied myself with various hobbies, including a few blissful evenings with Frederic. As always, he would try to persuade me to leave Sophia and join him, but I kept refusing.

One night comes to mind. It always stood out to me the most, a night unforgettable yet never mentioned until now.

At my estate, Frederic met me in the rose garden. He said, "I have something I want to show you now."

Taking me in his arms, we flew straight up as I held on as tightly as I could. As fast as lightning strikes, we arrived in the Ireland country side. I had no clue we could that!

It was amazing, the sculpture of the land. Though darkness was all around, I could see the beauty of it in the moonlight.

"This is my castle," he expressed as he opened his arms out to it.

The gray stone was dreary, gloomy yet peaceful.

Taking me inside the huge stone doors of the entrance, I was astonished at the beauty of the hall corridor that led to a great spatial relation with marble tile as green as emeralds. It was breathtaking. There were various weapons of war from every century you could imagine displayed throughout this room. Not paying attention to what Frederic had been doing at his desk, I was startled when he beckoned me to follow him. So far, this castle seemed shivery and moist. I followed him with my hand slightly in his as he led me to the tremendous spiraling staircase in the center of the castle. It was beautiful. The structure alone was so Viking, yet angelic.

Entering into his seductive bed chambers, I was taken back a step at the beauty inside this gigantic room of pleasure. The bed had deep red satin and what may have been pure silk sheets. There were velvet pillows that reminded me blood, so crimson and soft. I felt calm, strangely at ease, like I was home after many, many years of being away.

Slowly yet firmly, Frederic began kissing me, making me feel beautiful inside even though I was such evil. Unbuttoning my blouse, I felt his breath on my bare chest. Such feelings I thought I had lost. Before realizing it, we were both laying naked on his satin red sheets. No longer fighting the urge, I gave in to this lust. Afterwards, I fell into a deep, unsettling slumber.

The feeling of an unknown presence awoke me. Opening my eyes, I could vaguely see its teeth in the moonlight. They were long and white, pearly white, like an animal. Suddenly they were coming straight toward me, at my neck. Without thinking, I bolted to the nightstand gripping a dirty dagger that was barely visible on it. Thrusting this dagger into this thing's unknown heart, it looked at me with a shocked stature, like one who would turn to dust. It disappeared as fast as it had come upon me.

Stumbling back to the bed, I fell over, gasping for air like I was a mortal being. After getting my composure, I thought to myself, *What was on that dagger and who was that wretched Vampire-like creature who tried to kill me just now?*

As I pondered on this, still ordered across the bed, I realized I had just had an experience with "the Man." This was the first time he had been this close and tried to kill me. Still sensing this thing's presence nearby but only faintly, I rose from the bed, rushing down the masculine staircase in search of Frederic. Royally angered by now, I was ready for a fight and would not be caught off guard again. I yelled and yelled for Frederic out of agitation and a mixture of frustration. Finally, I heard his sweet voice…

"Bonjour," he said nonchalantly, almost amusingly. He appeared from the shadows of the darkness in the hallway corridor.

"Who was that? Was it 'the Man' you told me of?" I pleaded frightfully as I pointed in the upstairs direction.

"Whatever do you mean, my darling Annania? You look a fright. Let me calm your worries."

Taking me into his massive embrace, he made love to me with his mouth, and his hands caressed me entirely right there on this marble floor. Feeling such passion, I completely forgot about the horrid instance that had fallen upon me. His gentle yet controlling touch had me altogether hypnotized.

I stayed here with Frederic for only a night, but it was an amazing lustful time, except for the awful beast who tried to harm me. I explained it all to Frederic. He was vaguely maddened but not quite as upset as I would've hoped he'd been. We relaxed for hours it seemed and spoke of our futures together, knowing they were all lies, fantasies. Calm and at rest, I slipped off into a hard-physiological state. It felt to me like he stayed with me.

When I awoke the next evening, I was home in my coffin. Sophia was nowhere in sight. Maybe she was already out for the evening with her companion of late. I never told her of my experience that night at Frederic's castle. He and I agreed to never speak of it again.

Deciding to return to Alabama since it had been so long since we saw our plantation property, Sophia and I left our comfortable estate in Paris to the hands of our dear friend and lawyer, Frankie. Some time back, we had arranged for a cottage style home to be built on my parents' old plantation location. Yes, I kept this land all this time, just couldn't part with it. It was my raising. My home as a human. Of course, this house wasn't any comparison to our residence in Paris, but it was cozy, settling, and comforting. This was a change of pace and the scenery we needed now.

Putting our trust in a man called Collin, who we met sometime back in Switzerland, he accompanied us on our return to Alabama to help us and watch over us by day. Yes, he knew of us and what we were, how we kill others by draining them of their blood, yet he still seemed to love us, never questioning our methods. The poor guy was elderly and happened upon us in a darkened alleyway while we were passing through Switzerland, seeing more than he needed to see one night as we devoured two young men who were rapists of that area. After kidnapping him and bringing him back with us to Paris, he finally warmed up to us. Not sure why, but we just never had the heart to kill him. He was such a cute little man who made us laugh. He calls us his "strange, lovely girls." During these times I wonder if he really believed us to be vampires, or did he think we were just psychotic? Murderous? Killing for some human sport or something? Either way he's been a loyal friend to us thus far, and he also gets paid very well. He took perfect care of us all this time, and we love him for it. Oh, what someone can live with on their conscious with just the right amount of money!

Upon arriving, our cozy little cottage was lovely with a peacefulness about it. We were speechless at its beauty for such a small dwelling. The thick moss grew upward along the front of the place with flowers of assorted measure glowing in the moonlight along the path leading to the little Victorian style door. Homely windows covered with an array of dark curtains as to keep out the sunlight during the day. The mere sight of this intimate little home was just what we needed.

Sophia was still very acquainted with Anthony. He traveled ahead of us with his own arrangements and accommodations, so he could be close to her. In my opinion, he was too obsessed with her, always clinging or having to touch her in some fashion every time he was near her. It sickened me really.

Settling in our abode, we seemed peaceful for the most part. Sophia was showing signs of longing for her girl child to be made. Believe me, I felt awful from time to time just thinking about how I started all this and having to watch her go through such nonsense.

But I'm glad it's not me bearing this dreadful curse of having a baby.

Back to the story…

As I said, Sophia was getting extremely anxious yet somewhat nervous to sleep with Anthony. Who knew as a vampire such hormones still existed? As we laid together in our specially designed coffin, Sophia frightfully questioned, "Why does he have to die afterwards?"

Not answering her in reply, she already knew what the response would be. There wasn't a choice. It had to be done.

We slept. My dreams, or should I say my nightmares, came again…

Sophia was embracing Anthony in her arms tightly. He was dead. Upset and mournful, she was shouting at me, "It's all your fault, Annania!"

Trying to get to her as I ran but never getting close enough as she was seated on this bench outside, I could see her through our window of this diminutive room, but it would not open. She seemed so far away, yet she was right in front of me. All I could do while frozen at this horrible window was yell to her, "Sophia! Sophia! You'll die!"

The sun was starting to rise as she sat there on that miserable bench holding Anthony's lifeless body. She had no emotion about the fate of what was about to befall her. As the sun rose higher, her flesh began to burn turning into ashes as I watched her being tormented. In shock at this horrid scene, I was frozen, unable to move. As she screamed out in pain, she turned, looking up at me with hollow, cold eyes with the words, "You did this, it's your fault."

Trembling in a fearful state, I awoke, thinking, *Did I really lose my Sophia?* It seemed so real! But she was still laying right next me. Taking a breath of relief and staring numbly at the interior of my coffin, slowly calming myself, I finally snuggled back up to her.

Remembering one Easter weekend here in Alabama, Sophia and I visited a youth program at the local church. Curiously, we seated ourselves in the back on those uncomfortable pews that were a dreadful yellowish color so as not to be too noticeable. We experienced the reenactment of Christ on the cross dying for others' sins. It was very moving to see these individuals cry and quote scriptures from their Bible. Knowing that several of them were living in deceitful lies, the play itself was inspirational. As Sophia and I were taken back to our own memories of southern church services when we were children, we slipped out the back before it was over.

Sophia asked me as we approached our car, "What's going to be our fates? I mean, can we be forgiven?"

Not answering her as we drove away, I just shook my head, thinking to myself, *That will never be our destinies.*

Arriving home, we settled in our coffin somewhat early this night. We just couldn't feed on someone after watching such a dramatic display of love and sacrifice with an intense belief of the unknown.

"I wonder if Heaven really exists, Sophia. Seriously, I bet it would be beautiful. Part of me hopes we, someday, may see it. I don't know exactly, but maybe it's possible creatures like us could be forgiven. They portrayed tonight in the play repeatedly that 'all' could be forgiven for their sins. ...I strongly doubt it though, as we are condemned monsters who willingly want to kill. Oh, well, maybe there's a chance."

"Annania, let's leave fate in the hands of fate. I was speculative earlier after watching something so intense, but let us try not to figure this out on our own. It will drive into madness. I'm going to believe that one day we will see Heaven, even if we cannot stay there. I know we are damned, but I will keep the hope inside me that, while we were still mortal, we lived accordingly. Our souls, if we even have one, are evil. It's who we are now. Surely, as they've said for centuries, Christ loves us all. He has to understand who and what we are. It's beyond our power and knowledge. Now go to sleep."

After awakening one evening, we could sense the presence of "the Man." He felt to be close, but we couldn't actually see any evidence of his physical being. Not knowing when he would come at us, we definitely knew our time of peace was ending. It wouldn't be too much longer, and we would definitely have to return to Paris. Sophia had to get pregnant soon before something awful happened.

Standing near the window looking out at the moonlit sky, Sophia was gazing at the stars. With concern, I gently stood next to her with her hand in mine, caressing it. Tonight would be the night she made love to her beloved Anthony, still with thoughts in her head as to why we must kill him after the seed is planted.

"I feel I'm falling in love with him, Annania. He's going to be the father to my child. How could we just destroy him like he was never useful?"

"Forget 'love,' and do your duty. We are evil and will be throughout eternity. You need to vanish such thoughts and feelings from your mind."

Pondering a few seconds on my words, she stated, "Let's go. While I still have the courage to go through with this atrocious deception."

Frustrated, she went to the car. Who knew if it was frustration toward me or just at the entire situation. Driving fast down the winding road, Sophia never spoke a single word. As we headed to where Anthony was staying, we saw in the distance ahead of us, a man standing in the middle of the lane. Slowing to a complete halt, we could tell he was soaked from the heavy rain that was falling. Seeing from the headlights that he was tall and dark, wearing a black raincoat with a briefcase in his hand, he appeared to have noticeable scars on his face; he only stood there, ghost-like, not moving.

I dreaded getting out of the car to tell this idiot to remove himself from the road. Annoyed, I shouted to him, "Are you insane, mister? Do you want to die? Get out of the way!"

At that instant, I realized this wasn't some ordinary being.

"Sophia! It's 'the Man!' Get out of the car!"

She was already on her way towards me. How could we have been so oblivious to his presence?

At this moment, 'the Man' pulled a long dagger from this briefcase and was coming toward us as the case fell to the pavement. Bolting at him before he could approach us, we planted our fangs in his flesh. Strong and fierce, it seemed he wasn't at all human. Feeling like I've experienced this familiar blood before as we tried to drain him of all he had, he gripped me by the back of my head holding firmly to my hair as he slung me to the side of the road.

Stumbling, I regrouped, and as I darted back to him, he swiftly turned and stabbed Sophia in her neck with that pointed dagger. In anguish, she fell to the pavement. As I got closer to him, he swung back and planted the knife right into my side just under my ribcage. Dropping to the ground, I crawled hastily over to Sophia who lay helpless. Was this the end? How could this be? These thoughts flooded my brain. What was that dagger, and how could it hurt us in this way?

This being was moving in closer to us laughing as we pleaded to him to leave us alone. Right when he lifted his arm to finish us off, someone snatched his whole body up in the air tossing him across to the ditch in front of us. Trying to see through the heavy rainfall, I wondered who could have saved us. In that instant, I laughed out loud with joy and relief as I saw Frederic. He picked us up holding us steady as he helped us back to the vehicle. Feeling like I was slowly dying, I knew this being had weakened us with the knife. To this day, I cannot understand as to why this weapon had such an effect on us.

Sophia was bleeding and losing a lot of blood by this point. Frederic went back to the ditch where he threw "the Man," but he was gone. Taking us back to our cottage, Frederic didn't speak a word to us. As he placed us both on the bed with blood everywhere, he finally said, "Bandage yourselves. You will be weak but you will not die. Sleep a few nights, and I will see you then."

He was then gone as fast as he came.

Sophia appeared to be getting weaker as I struggled to get dressing for our wounds. Placing with grace, I helped her to our sleeping quarters. In pain and scared with tear-filled eyes as we drifted in and out of slumber, I quoted softly in French the verse from the Christian

Bible, John 3:16. It was the first thing to come into my mind at that moment.

> *Car Dieu a tant aime le monde qu'll adonne son*
> *Fils unique, a fin que quiconque croit en lui ne*
> *Perrisse point, mais qu'll ait la vie eternelle.*

Almost in a whisper she asked, "Are you sure we aren't dying?"

"We are not going to die. You're just delusional from the loss of so much blood. Have you forgotten? We are going to live forever. Now shut up, and let's just sleep."

All the while, I pondered if "the Man" was who I encountered in Ireland. Could it be him? It frightened me to think about this, so I cleared my mind despite the excruciating pain I was in and fell into the deepest sleep I've ever experienced. Sleeping so tightly intertwined, it felt as if we were one being.

My dreams returned…

Sophia and I were alone in the garden. We were only small children. Bleeding from the wound in her neck, she stared at me impotently. There was no way to stop the trauma. Appearing and disappearing all around us in a circular fashion, "the Man" was laughing and chanting at me, "She's dying! It's all your fault!"

As he repeated these words louder and louder, I yelled at him to stop and just leave us in peace. Suddenly in a flash, we were grown now with Sophia vanishing from my arms. I was crying out for help, but no one came to my distress call. Darkness closed in all around me. I could not see anything. I only heard the voice of "the Man" chanting at me as before. Maddening me. I became so afraid, wanting him to stop with these words. In that moment, I saw him in front of me in this vast darkness. He reached for me with the dagger pointed to my throat. I awoke.

Shaking, but only vaguely, I glanced over to Sophia who was sleeping soundly, and kissed her forehead. Calming myself, I relaxed and drifted back to an emotional state of numbness.

Two nights had passed as I awakened, slipping out of our casket, to find Frederic reclining in a chair across the room. As Sophia still slumbered, I casually walked over to him. Thanking him and apologizing for being off my guard, I asked, "How did you know we were in trouble? I thought you were still in Paris somewhere?"

"My darling Annania, you know I always know where you are. You are my creation, are you not? I can always feel you."

"Amazing," I replied.

"We can do many things since we are connected. Feeling your pain is one of them."

Glancing at my side, I noticed it was entirely healed.

"Sophia seems to be weakened still. I'm so glad you showed up when you did. I have so many questions I need answered. Who is this guy, and why does he want us dead?"

"Darling, she may need to rest a little longer. Her wound was very deep, it seemed. She will heal completely in time. You should both feed when she wakes. It will strengthen you."

Interrupting him, I asked, "Why was the blade on his knife so painful to us? Why did it weaken us to the point we felt as if we were dying? This was a strange experience for me so far. It kind of frightens me."

"I'm not quite sure, my love, but it probably had an extreme amount of silver in its blade. Silver will dampen us. It doesn't blend with our blood. I know, my darling, this is confusing to you as to why, but 'the Man' has chased our kind for centuries."

"Is he human? It surely didn't feel like he was," I stated boldly.

"No, my dear, he's not exactly human anymore. More like what you would call a half-vampire. One who hasn't yet drank the blood of a mortal. One who refused the blood in return from their maker. Only having the strength of an immortal, yet he can still live forever. He's definitely a dangerous creature."

As he spoke these words to me, he gazed blankly in thought out the small window like he wasn't really here with me in this conversation.

Disturbing us, a knock came at the front door. It was Anthony. Collin was letting him in, seating him on the cute lovers' sofa in the parlor. Before I could turn to go greet Anthony, Frederic stood, grabbing me in his masculine arms kissing me quickly on my lips. He disappeared hastily through my window after whispering to me in my ear "I love you, my darling, Annania. Please stay aware of 'the Man.' Stay safe."

Speechless, I stood there a few seconds, tasting him on my lips. Feeling aroused and warm, I knew I had to shake this feeling. I have so much passion for that vampire.

Wiping my lips with my sleeve, I went to find out what the hell Anthony was doing here.

Sipping a glass of sweet tea as I came up to him, I asked rather boldly, "What are you doing here?"

"I need to see Sophia. I miss her, and she never showed up for our dinner the other night. Just got a terrible feeling, and I need to see her," responded Anthony in a frustrated tone.

"She's fine," I snapped. "You can't see her tonight. She's not feeling well."

Before he could protest, Sophia came into the parlor toward him. Covered in a stained scarf about her neck, she still felt feeble. Rolling my eyes in agitation as she gave me a biting glance, I made my presence scarce. I made my way into the kitchen. Collin was at the dinette table and removed himself to his bedchambers as I came in. That's just like Collin to stay to his own business, never asking questions.

Thwarted, I decided to drink early tonight, so I left in hunt for my next victim. *Maybe,* thinking to myself, *I will devour several innocent living things tonight. After all I deserve the pleasure after what I've been through these past few nights.* Even having self-pity, I could still enjoy breaking a few necks this wretched night. Quoting out loud as I strolled the old back street, "Come out and play with me, you despicable souls."

Meanwhile, Sophia and Anthony were snuggling and drowning in affection like lovers do on the little couch, repeating over and over how much they'd missed each other in the last couple of days. That's when he noticed the blood-stained scarf about her throat. Seeing the concern on his face she promptly said, "I fell on an old ax in the tool shed. Stupid thing really, I tripped over some cords and landed on the tip of an ax. Luckily it wasn't as bad as it could have been. Besides, it's only a scratch. Now kiss me, you fool."

They'd been so intensely wrapped up in each other's arms, Anthony totally forgot to question her story. Making their way to the little guest room down the hall, she whispered in his ear, "I must have you now."

Kissing and caressing each other like some kind of pornographic film, he removed her blouse revealing her porcelain breasts. As he kissed and teased her, they fell back onto the undersized bed. Within moments, the seed was self-sowed. Throwing him from her he landed in the floor, stunned.

"It's done. You're no longer needed," she expressed.

Seeing her sharp fangs begin to show, he knew he was in trouble. Her eyes were reddened, and she looked like something undead. He knew she wasn't human now. Jumping to his feet in fear as he tried to pull his trousers up, he made his way to the exit. She was on him before he could cross the threshold. Struggling, fighting, he gave it all he had to defend himself against this monster he thought he loved.

She drained him of all his blood. Collin could hear the commotion from his room but dared not to open his door to investigate. He only turned his volume up on his radio that sounded through his headphones and relaxed into his pillow.

Stopping, Sophia looked at his face in her hands as his body went limp and tumbled to floor.

"I did love you, but it has to be this way. I had no choice."

She was still holding Anthony's lifeless body when I returned home. With an evil grin, I wickedly sniffed the air smelling the aroma of his blood. Aw, such a sweet scent. His blood was still warm in his body, so I rushed over to them and buried my teeth into his throat. Sophia cursorily shoved me away as she dropped his hideous body. With slight tears in her eyes she got up and put her blouse back on, removing the scarf from her neck. The wound was completely healed.

Scanning about the room, there was blood everywhere it seemed. His blood was even on our facials. I licked my lips slowly in relief, already knowing the answer to the question I was about to ask, "Is it done?"

"Yes, it's done. It's over," Sophia responded softly.

Hurriedly, we started to clean everything, getting towels from the linen closet and showering. We finally had it all done, spotless.

As we dressed ourselves, Sophia said, "I'm pregnant. I can feel it inside me. It's weird yet I'm excited. Still wished he could have lived. But it's completed, and I'm glad. I can't believe I lost control of myself the way I did. It brought out the demon in me."

Not really listening to this whining, I took her hand and led her to our resting place. Kissing her forehead, I sweetly said to her, "Sleep now. It's over. I'll be right back. I got to dispose of his body."

Sophia was asleep by the time I got back. Climbing in beside her, I held her close to me as I drifted into angelic abyss. Strangely, I slept in sweet serenity this night. No dreams.

With time moving at what seemed like an eternity during Sophia's pregnancy, we eventually adapted well to her new condition. Collin was astonished that a vampire who is considered dead could actually conceive and carry a baby. Amazingly, this child inside her could survive on blood alone.

So far, this seemed to be going quite easily. Sophia seemed to be moody yet happy.

Wasn't I wrong! I never dreamed she could get so ugly, so grouchy!

With Sophia getting closer to delivery of her girl child, she mostly stayed to herself, quiet. Sleeping by day and lounging around by night, barely feeding on anyone. Of course, we still shared our coffin, but it was much tougher now with her being so irritable. I would be glad when this thing was over and my Sophia was back to normal. She was so cranky when she wasn't silent, always yelling at poor Collin. There was just no pleasing her. If I didn't love her so much, I would have killed her myself!

Not really hungering for human blood, she was actually fine without it at this point. She mostly drank the chicken blood we bought at the grocery store. This was amazing to me! How could a vampire carry a child and survive only on blood, yet alone chicken blood, and the child still seem healthy? Yet, how can a vampire live on just blood for an eternity? It amazes me.

Finally, the night came. Sophia's girl child was to be born. The night seemed to be at peace, except for Sophia, who lay on the bed propped up on pillows and blankets. Looking absolutely miserable, she had blood sweats, and her skin steamed from the heat inside her. Breathing heavily at a fast pace she really did look monstrous.

As I sat beside her I asked, "Are you okay? Are ready for this?" My question was obviously a mistake. Her response made me jump in fear but only a little.

"Shut up, Annania! Leave me be! When this is over, I'm going to kill you! How could it hurt me this bad?! I'm a vampire! It's not supposed to be this way!"

I swear I think she even growled at me. Leaving the room and leaving her in the hands of Collin, I mumbled under my breath somewhat angrily, "Not if I kill you first, you pitiful creature."

Standing near her at the end of the bed, Collin raised the blankets telling her to, "Push! Here it comes!"

Rushing back into the room, I could actually see the child's head peeking out of her, blood falling every-where while she screamed in pain. The blood was slightly tempting but at least it wasn't as strong as the scent of human blood.

Unbelievably, this whole scene was making me nau-seous, hungry for blood. Simply too much blood. Notic-ing my fangs were starting to contract, I decided it was best for me to just leave the room.

Promptly, I went outside to our little flower garden in the back, placing myself on the white wooden bench. Calming my actions, I thought of Frederic, wishing he was here beside me. Sophia's screams continued mak-ing me jump a few times in worry as they interrupted my imaginings of my lover, who I missed greatly at this moment.

Dreaming of being in his embrace, I lost all contact with the sounds around me, such a beautiful bliss I was in now. The immortal lustful thoughts of my soulless mate caressing my body with sweet yet gentle touch while I slowly kissed his neck…

Then suddenly my visions disappeared. This strange noise behind me caught my curiosity. A dark mysterious shadow moved across the side of the house near the hedge bushes, catching my full attention. Instinct set in as I speedily darted for this dark being, seizing it by its throat. As I struggled with this strong creature of the night, I could see vaguely its face in the pale moonlight. That's when I recognized it was "the Man."

Noticing he already had his dagger coming straight for my temple, I pulled from his grip in fear. Coming at me, he had a horrible look about him as stumbled backwards sailing over the hedges. As he approached me, I jumped up at him baring my teeth into his flesh. Dropping his dagger to the ground he swiftly turned me around throwing my entire being across the grass.

Breathlessly, I lay on the moistened grass trying to see him. Hastily he picked up his knife as he approached me. Still winded, I tried to gain the strength to attack again. But before I could act, he was already standing over me with his weapon aimed at my chest.

To my surprise, he suddenly halted, and looking at me with his dark hollow eyes, he said, "You must die tonight. I'm sorry, but it must be this way."

I knew this meant Sophia as well. I could see his hatred for vampires in his eyes as he hovered over me. But why such hatred?

At this moment, he raised his hand to deliver the final blow to my chest. Strengthening myself, I leaped to my feet sinking my fangs as deep as I could into the side of his head. Seeing his past, his fears, his hatred for our kind as I drank his blood, trying my best to drain him of all his life.

In this vision, I could see that a vampire had badly wronged him, leaving him for dead, his family tortured and left dying right in front of him. But before I could envision more, I felt a tight grip on my neck as I was surprisingly cast aside, slamming into the side of the cottage, seemingly I felt as if I had been knocked out.

Coming to, I saw daybreak as it was hitting my eyes. Cursorily, I searched as fast as I could all around the house before daylight would fully come. No trace was found of this man. My mind went straight to Sophia. Had he got her? Why wasn't I dead? He could have finished me while I was out.

Entering my room where I left Sophia earlier, Collin was relaxing beside her as she held a beautiful baby girl in her arms, all snuggled up nicely in a cotton blanket. Calming myself before walking over to her, I took a few deep breaths. Leaning into them, I saw a tiny creature, a lovely fragile little girl with huge green eyes and slightly blonde hair. Noticing how glowingly happy

Sophia seemed, I totally forgot about the horrible experience with "the Man." It was finally over for her. No more of this immortal, physical pain.

Gazing at this picturesque bundle of pure joy, I thought to myself, *Who says vampires cant have feelings?*

As I stood there, my mind began to think of "the Man." There was no reasoning why he hadn't killed us this night. Maybe I did drain him more than I felt. Maybe he was weakened. I almost had a feeling of pity for him after seeing vaguely some his past. Vanishing these thoughts, Collin was removing the baby from Sophia's arms, taking her ever so graciously to his room. I suppose he knew what to do with it.

As day was coming through the window, I helped Sophia over to our coffin. Climbing in I saw she was wondering why I looked so roughed up with grass all over me and blood still stained on my lips.

After a few moments as we relaxed in our abode, she asked, "Did you have a tough victim tonight?"

"Yes, you could say that. But it's okay now. Just go to sleep."

I never told Sophia of that night and what I encountered, of how we were almost destroyed. Although it still haunts me as to why he spared us.

As we lay sleeping, you guessed it, my dreams returned...

Sophia was in anguish as she lay there having her baby. Screaming, I tried to plead with her to run. "The

Man" was standing next to her as he began stabbing her repeatedly with his mystifying dagger. On the floor, I could see the girl child lying dead on some blankets. Collin was crying as he sat beside this child. "The Man" turned his direction to Collin as he threw him at my feet, blood pouring from his lifeless body. Coming toward me, this atrocious being snarled at me with intent of killing me. Sophia was shouting at me, "It's all your fault!"

Her words haunted me over and over till it seemed like a chant. As this echo of her words repeated, "the Man" firmly grabbed my arm as he stabbed me several times, saying, "You must die!"

His eyes were so hollow, void, just sad as I gazed into them. I felt as if I were dying. Sophia's words continued to ring in my ears as I was slowing fading away. I awoke…

This nightmare continued several nights after. It kept reoccurring, only the voice of Sophia would get louder, deafening. What does it mean? I may never know. Never understanding. Like I said, it has to be my eternal torment.

Over time, we all had to make adjustments. Kelli was now a toddler. Very beautiful and petite. Her green eyes sparkled under her lovely, flowing, curly hair. She was a little stubborn and bold at times, but we loved her. Collin took care of her most of the time, especially by day. He proved to be a very respected "nanny."

Sophia and I decided not to tell Kelli about who we are until she could understand it. Collin began schooling her at home throughout the days.

Kelli was growing fast. She started to ask many questions about where she came from and who was her father. Never giving any answers, we always cut her off or changed the subject.

Seeing Anthony in her, I could see Sophia as well. Although she seemed bolder than them at times, braver. Almost like me! Her attitude showed signs of devilish behavior and love. She definitely was one of a kind.

When Kelli was experiencing teenage mannerism, she was a knockout! Curly hair and a lot longer, she was becoming taller than any of us. I'm guessing it was from her father.

Still living in our cottage in Alabama, we hadn't had any trouble from "the Man" during the raising of Kelli. But sometimes from a distance, we sensed his presence, knowing he was watching us. Collin was aging, almost like a grandfather. Kelli always called him "Grandpapa."

Frederic would pay little visits from time to time, but never interfered in our affairs. He would only remind me of the curse and how it needed to be carried out.

Kelli's questions started coming more and more. She was more persistent. Sophia tried avoiding her, not talking about any of it. I kept telling Sophia she has to know. We couldn't keep it from her any longer.

One late evening, Kelli came to me demanding to know the truth, the secrets that we were hiding from her. She wanted to know the answers to where she came from, who her father was, and why must we always sleep during the day and never dine with her at dinner. Why weren't we like Collin? And why hasn't she ever been able to go make friends and be around normal people?

Sophia was out already to feed this night, so I motioned for her to be seated next to me on my little loveseat. Frustrated, I set my book down and placed my hand on hers and stated, "Okay, ask me, and I will be honest with you. Yes, we have secrets."

"Why, Annania, do you only come out of your room at night? Does my mother stay in there with you all day? And why is there no answer during the day when I call out to y'all from the door? Oh, and why the hell is there a huge lock on your door?"

Before I could answer she began again, "Why doesn't mother ever speak of my father? Who is my father? Dammit, why do I have a strange craving for the chicken blood in the fridge? Am I weird or messed up? This isn't normal! Tell me something!"

Agitated, I decided to tell her the truth whether she could handle it or not. I only hoped Sophia would understand.

"Calm down, Kelli. I'll explain it all, but you must not interrupt me. Just listen. Believe all I tell you. It's going to seem unreal, but honestly it is our reality."

Letting go of her hand, I began telling her the entire story from the very beginning. As far back as when it began for Sophia and I. I told her of our home in Paris, of Frederic, of Sophia and Victor, of the curse upon us all, and finally of her father, Anthony.

"You killed my father?" she asked almost in a whisper as she stared to the floor beneath her feet.

"We had to, Kelli. It was the only way. Now be quiet, and I can tell you more. As I've said, you're the curse now. It all weighs on your shoulders. No longer is it your mother's burden to bear, but yours. You must repeat the same steps as your mother, or we could all be destroyed. I was freed of this curse when I turned your mom. If I could change the past, I would. But it's done now. The time is close where you have to make a decision, a choice. Remain a human and live a normal life or become what we are, a vampire. But you must know before you decide, our fates rest in your decision. A human life means our destruction. A few nights from now, we will be returning to Paris. You'll love it there. You haven't had the pleasure of meeting my beloved Frederic, but you will soon enough. He suggests it all be completed at our estate rather than here. I realize it's a lot of information to take in all at once, but try to understand."

Speechless, she sat there seemingly confused; it was not exactly what she was expecting to hear. Strangely, I could see she believed me, but her feelings toward our fates was concerning me. I didn't care how she felt about me at this point, but Sophia didn't deserve to be hated. Kelli was about to speak when Sophia busted through the door after hearing the latter part of our conversation. Her expression wasn't at all cheerful toward me. Looking straight at her mother, Kelli leapt to her feet and said sarcastically "Well, that explains the hunger for the chicken blood."

Passing by her mom, Kelli kissed her cheek as she went back to her room. Sophia was speechless but only for a second. Placing herself beside me she asked, "Did you tell her everything? About Anthony? The curse? About us?"

"Yes, I did. Right from the beginning. You know as much as I do that she needed to hear it. It was better for her to know than to wait until that night to try and explain it."

"I know. It's the right thing to do, but it pains me so much just to talk of it all. How did she take the news? Does she hate us now? Or does she just blame you?"

"I'm not sure. You came in, and that was it. We will find out soon enough, though, I'm pretty sure. Guess we will know our destiny soon, now won't we?"

Before Sophia could respond, I arose and left for town. I needed blood, lots of it!

We made arrangements and were on our way back to Paris. Sadly, Collin enigmatically passed away before we left. We did have a small ceremony for him, burying him in the little old cemetery of the local church.

Frederic agreed to meet us upon on our return. Thankfully Kelli watched over by day as we sailed back to Paris. Yes, we were still old fashioned and never took planes. She barely spoke to either of us but at least she stayed loyal.

Arriving at our estate a little before night, it was an endearing, cool evening. Kelli was amazed at its beauty. She never realized we were so wealthy. As we piled out of the limo, Kelli noticed a dark-haired man leaning over the hedge bushes. Smiling, he walked over to us as if to greet us. His eyes met Kelli's immediately. This was going to mean trouble for us, I'm sure of it. As we entered the home, Frederic met us giving us a wonderful welcome.

Upon our first night back, I strolled my grounds while the others talked in the study. They were getting more acquainted with Frederic and discussing more in detail about the estranged curse. I grew tiresome of all the chatter. As I gazed at the stars and such, I heard a faint cry of what seemed to be a cat. Walking over to the large rose bush, underneath were two kittens. Black and gray with white stripes. They were adorable. Hissing at me as I picked them up, I carried them back to my room, up the winding staircase. Sophia was going to strangle, me but I was keeping them. I named them Louie and Jasmine. Needless to say, I kept them and soon turned them into little vampire cats. I know it was crazy, but I had to see what would happen if I changed them. Yes, they are very mean to others but gentle with us, only us. Sophia and I are the only ones who can handle them. I cannot let them out of my room. I feed them animal blood because human blood would be too much for them. They sleep with me and Sophia in our coffin most of the time. Couldn't imagine this life without them now.

Okay, now back to my story…

After speaking to Frankie, we learned the man's name was Derrek. Apparently, he was her nephew who she hired, with our money of course, to keep the grounds up. He also stays in the lower wing of the mansion.

The night was soon forthcoming when Kelli would have to make a sincere choice. Derrek and Kelli were becoming close, almost like a relationship. You never saw one without the other. It was making me fearful yet angered at the mere thought of her falling in love with this guy. This mortal. How would he affect her decision? Frederic even says he's suspicious of him, but it was my call as to what to do with him. Believably, Kelli warmed up to Frederic. Almost like a father figure. He was staying around, but not too close, probably until this whole mess was past us. Finally, one night in the garden, Frederic and Kelli had been leisurely walking and talking about pointless information when he seated her beside him on the small bench. He begun to explain in more detail about the curse upon her. He spoke of how the curse was upon her and how it would also follow her, depending on the choice she made.

In a charming, seductive fashion he said, "In a few nights from now, my pretty child, you'll have to make this final decision. Human or to be immortal? As a human, you will die someday a terrible death, but as a vampire, as we are now, you can quench that blood thirst feeling you've been having and live forever, never dying. Upon the wrong choice, it will destroy the ones you love. You'll have their blood on your hands. Can you live a human existence knowing you murdered your family? No need to answer me, just ponder on that. This very spot we are now will be the place for your decision. When the time comes your instinct will lead you on the right path.

"Of course, your human body will die if you choose the way of a vampire, but you will live with a new, immortal body. Human blood will be your only source of nourishment. The blood will be your only peace, your only satisfaction. Along with the curse that will be passed onto you. You'll then have to find a male human to conceive a girl child by, same as your mother did. This curse must continue for the sake of our kind. You must understand fully all of this that is placed upon you. Our fates are in your hands now."

Not knowing what to say to all she just heard, Kelli seemed to be in deep thought. She finally spoke, "How could I ever drink blood? Murder a person? And what of Derrek?"

"You cannot tell Derrek any of this. It will only make for confusion. He will die someday. You will not. You see, my pretty girl, it cannot work between you. It's best to forget about him, no matter how much you think you love him. Unless you would wish a horrible fate upon him. Do you understand my words, Kelli?"

Anger settled in her as she stood not saying a word. She walked slowly away from Frederic, thinking to herself about Derrek. Making her way to Derrek's room, she joined him on his bed as he lay there watching his television. She couldn't help but ponder all of what Frederic said to her. All the while, as she snuggled in close to Derrek, she kept thinking, *I love him and I am going to enjoy him for as long as I possibly can. It's all their fault I was born into this whole mess. I blame Annania more than my mother, since she gave this dreadful curse to us.*

Curling in closer to her lover she pushed the thoughts from her mind.

During that whole conversation between Frederic and Kelli, Sophia and I were eavesdropping. We both contemplated whether or not she would accept her fate and ours. Surely she wouldn't destroy us all.

Tensions flared in the air over the next few nights. We sent Frankie to Venice on a paid vacation for a month or so just to get her out of the house. Kelli wasn't really speaking to any of us except Derrek. She passed by us without even a glance. I could see how she cared for that boy, and it worried me. I knew he would become trouble for us during all this. Sending him away wouldn't solve anything; besides, she would go with him. It did no good to mention to her to just leave him alone. It'd just anger her all the more. Time would tell what her beloved Mr. Derrek's fate will become.

The night before the big decision, I was alone in the kitchen when I heard an awful noise near the back door. Knowing everyone was out for the evening, I just couldn't get over the feeling I was being watched. And now there was this strange bumping at the door. Rushing cautiously to the door, I peeked around the seal but saw nothing. Befuddled, I walked tardily back to the bar stool sitting down. As I finished my letter to my editor, the back door suddenly slammed shut. Turning cursorily, "the Man" was standing right in front of me. Yes, I was taken back, frightened. Noticing there was no dagger in his hands, Instinct was telling me to kill him now before he had a chance to take me out, but I couldn't move. I felt drawn to him, to his sadness. Face to face with him now, he moved slightly closer. Feeling his breath on my chin, I wanted to run away.

Finally I mustered up the courage to speak, "Why haven't you just killed us? Kill me now if you must but quit haunting me! "

I remembered what Frederic told me about "the Man," that he only wanted to kill us all, but I'm not so sure about that at this moment. Seeing such pain in his eyes, he just stared at me. So frightful and sad.

He spoke, "Annania, I must talk with you. I've been waiting for some time now, just watching you. I think I know you now. You were the only one to see my past as it really was. And how much I hate the creature you are. I'm not going to kill you for now, nor your friends. I want you to know my side, my story first. To understand my pain. No time to begin a story like mine at this moment, but I will return soon. As for your beloved Frederic, he is a devil, evil. I will destroy him one day."

"But why? Why must you hurt my precious Frederic? I don't comprehend any of this. Why do you hate us so much?"

"In time, you will see," he responded as leaned in closer, kissing my forehead.

I could smell the fresh scent of blood running through his veins yet it vaguely smelled of Frederic.

"There's something about you Annania that intrigues me. I've decided to not harm your estranged lover for now. I can feel the love you have for him, but that will change. I once loved him, too, until... Well, you'll know soon enough. I'll be watching you, Annania." He spoke these words so softly in my ear as he raised his head, kissing my lips. I suddenly pulled away from him as my eyes closed with this exotic feeling pulsing through me when his warm lips touched mine.

So intrigued by this kiss, it made me all the more confused.

Opening my eyes from this feeling of ecstasy, he was gone.

Paralyzed, I sat there in a state of silence, thinking to myself, *What do I make of all he told me? Who is he? His name? Where's he from? Why is he torturing me in this way?*

Knocking me from my thoughts, the front door slammed. Frederic and Sophia were coming inside. Bouncing to my feet, I went to the front parlor to greet them. Still somewhat shaken, Frederic noticed something was alienated. Kelli and Derrek plundered through the door about the time Frederic was going to speak. Passing by us as fast as they came in, up the staircase they went with not a care in the world as to what we were up to.

Frederic took my hand in his as he leaned in, kissing me slowly, passionately. Following him into the study, we placed ourselves together on the cozy loveseat in the corner. Surprisingly, Sophia fell in behind us in the arched doorway just rolling her eyes at us. After a couple of seconds, she gracefully turned and shimmied up the stairs.

Frederic finally spoke, "What's wrong with you, my darling Annania? You look as if you've seen your death."

"I'm fine now. Just a small encounter with 'the Man' a few moments ago. He spooked me in the kitchen, but he's no longer there. He said some crazy things to me that have me a little bewildered. I get a slight fearsome feeling knowing he's out there just watching us. Wish I knew what he wanted from us."

Frederic replied aggravated, "He wants to murder us all. He's insane! Nothing but trouble. I should have disposed of him centuries ago."

"What exactly are you saying? He did speak of knowing you, even loving you once. You have to explain this to me."

"Like I said, he's insane, very sick creature. Annania, he only wants to cause trouble for us. If you must know, I knew him. Several moons ago in the dirty alleys of Paris, I met him. He's called Samuel. Only a teenager then, I took him in. He was pitiful, starving. I fed him, cared for him. As he grew older, I even loved him. So much that I needed him to be with me for eternity, trying on several occasions to get him to allow me to turn him and be with me always, but he refused every time. I cannot turn someone unless they are willing.

"Angrily one evening I was pleading with him again. I became so agitated I lost my temper and attacked him. After piercing his neck I realized what I had done. I tried to convince him to drink from me now and live, but he still refused. I thought he would die at this point. I had drained him to the point of death but he only refused me. So I left him there to die, and I never looked back. Over time, I kept my distance from him, peering at him out of curiosity. He should have died that night but he lived. He only got stronger, never dying, never hungering for blood. My blood obviously still exists in his veins. Has to be what is keeping him alive. Since then, he's always had this hatred for me. Blames me for all his bad experiences, his pain. He's vowed to me several times that he would kill me one day. But so far, he's not prevailed."

"So, you're the reason why he wants to kill all our kind. Frederic, why didn't you tell us this sooner? Oh, never mind. I've had enough. I'm tired, and this conversation is starting to bore me." Glancing back at Frederic as I proceeded to the doorway, he was reclined back on the little sofa, so seductive. Harshly I stated, "He won't hurt me."

Peering up at me with a cross concerned look, he just squinted his nose at me. Slyly, playfully, I eased back over to him kissing him as I whispered, "I love you no matter the past. You are bound to me for all eternity."

Turning to make my exit, Frederic replied in a faint whisper, "I love you, my darling Annania."

Reaching the staircase, I decided to linger in my own miserable thoughts for a while. So, I made my way to the deserted beach near the rocks. Lingering here for what seemed like hours, I just watched the ocean waves slam against the shore and listened to the wind howling so aggressively. Feeling it on my face was peaceful. Seeing the lightning flash across the horizon was breathtaking. Standing in amazement that a creature such as I could have a place in God's creation, I tilted my head upward as the rain began to sprinkle down. Feeling the coolness of it on my face, I was unwillingly interrupted. This young couple had eased up behind me. In my own bliss, I did not sense them. Seeing me in this bright moonlit rainy night, they saw me for what I was.

With fangs fully out, I quickly moved toward them. Running away, they screamed out for help. Attacking them both, I fed on them until there was no life left in them. Dropping their lifeless bodies to the ground, I contemplated on whether to leave them there or get rid of the evidence. Deciding to drag them to the water, I threw the bodies as far as I had strength to toss them. It thrilled me to consider the fact that these wretched bodies would soon wash up to some shore with no one knowing what happened to them, or maybe the sharks would get to enjoy a meal. Either way, it served them right for interrupting my self-indulgence. Slightly laughing to myself, I thought, *Although, such a sweet coincidence that my dinner came to me.*

Noticing daybreak was setting in, I hurriedly made my way back home.

Approaching the cobblestone walkway in back, I overheard Kelli in the garden with Derrek. It sounded like he was proposing to her, asking her to move away with him to London. Becoming furious, this set off a rage of anger in me. Impulsively, I disturbed their little romantic setting.

"Derrek, leave us. I need to speak with Kelli."

Glancing toward me while he stood there holding her hand, he kissed her forehead and made his way back inside. I could tell she wasn't very thrilled to see me. Trying to walk away from me, I sternly grabbed her wrist turning her back around. Holding her, I asked boldly, "Are you crazy? You know you can't marry him! You know the reasons why!"

"I can do whatever I want! If I want to spend my life with him, then I will! I have a choice, remember. I do not have to be like you, like my mother. I can live a normal life if I so choose."

Pulling away from my grip, she stomped back the house. Speechless, I stood there feeling more infuriated than before. Thinking aloud, "Who does he think he is? Trying to ruin our future. Our mere existence! He can't have Kelli!"

Maddened beyond belief, I made my way straight to Derrek. I found him all relaxed on the leather couch in the sitting room listening to his headphones. Stunned as I came near, he was quite fearful at the sight of me. Fangs showing and rage in my eyes, I snatched him from his comfortable position tossing him to the cold tile floor. The more he cried out in anguish, the more it excited me.

Struggling to free himself from my tight grasp, I buried my teeth into his vein. Drinking until I just could not take in any more, I dropped his limp body from my embrace. Carrying him out to the small cemetery behind our estate as fast as I could, I dumped him in a small tomb with a concrete door. As I pulled the heavy stone door to a close, I said with an evil grin, "Now you are where you belong."

Entering the kitchen, Frederic was seated at the bar reading a Chinese cookbook. Hearing me come in, he said, "You know, I can't eat any of these recipes but it all sounds quite delicious."

Chuckling to myself, I seated myself next to him. He looked up at me smiling and stated, "You've just drank, haven't you? I can smell the fresh aroma of blood."

"I have. It was by far the best I've had in many years, apart from yours, my love."

"Oh, really. Then why do I sense you've done something really devilish, my darling Annania?" he asked with a slight grin.

"Because I have, my love. It had to be done. I drained Derrek of his blood this night. His tiresome body is laying in the graveyard."

"I see," said Frederic. "I do believe it's best, my darling. He was only going to bring turmoil to us. Kelli needed to be free of him for our sake. But now, my darling, what do you mean to tell Kelli?"

"Not sure just yet. But I will think of the right thing to say. It will work out, you'll see, my love."

"You never cease to surprise me, my darling Annania. I knew you would not let that wretched boy stop us."

Leaning over and kissing his lips softly, I stated, "Let's not mention this to Sophia just yet. She'll be furious at me."

"Your secret is safe within me, my darling. I leave this mess in your hands," he said sweetly, kissing my cheek as he rose to leave.

With cookbook in hand, he faded out into night.

I was pondering my actions of the night with my face in my hands and elbows on bar when Sophia came strolling in placing herself next to me.

"I just saw Frederic walking toward the garden with a cookbook to his face," Sophia said.

"Yes, he's weird like that. Still love him though."

We both laughed.

"You okay?" Sophia asked, concerned. "I feel like something is wrong. You look as if you have stuff on your mind. So much going on lately, I feel we never talk much anymore."

"Oh, I'm fine, Sophia. Just a rough struggle with my victim tonight. Seemingly, this has been a long sort of night for me."

"Do you happen to know what's bothering Kelli? I know she is angry at us lately, but she seems all the more so tonight. She rushed past earlier like she was crying. Would not even speak a word to me when I yelled to her. Just went straight to her room, slamming the door behind her."

"She's probably just angry at me, as usual," I responded. "We will discuss it later. Seriously, don't worry about her. She'll be fine."

"If you say so..." Sophia stated slowly as she gestured for me to follow. "I am a little tired now, rest would be wonderful at this point."

Smiling as Sophia took my hand in hers, I fell in behind her as we made our way to our resting place.

Meanwhile, Frederic was resting in the garden before sunlight was to set in, still studying his cookbook. Samuel suddenly appeared right in front of him. Not bothered by his presence, Frederic just raised his eyes up over his book picking at him. Calmly yet aggravated, he asked, "What do you want now? Can't you just stay away? I gave you a castle all your own in Ireland. Can't you just go back there?"

"I will tell Annania the truth about us, why I hate you so dearly. I'll even tell her what really happened to her family in Alabama. She must know the truth and what kind of monster you really are."

"Feel free to tell her whatever you like. Our love is strong. She won't believe you entirely anyways. You know as well as I do it can never be the same between you and I. Centuries have passed since we were in Ireland. Too much has happened. I tried only to make you immortal, you know this. But you wanted me dead, gone. I cannot keep allowing you to live if you do not go away and stay away," Frederic stated very sternly.

"You hated me long before I could remember. Your hate started the day you attacked me and left me for dead. I will put an end to you Frederic. Before my time is done, you will be obliterated."

"I will await that day with pure excitement, my boy. My strength exceeds yours, so why must you continue to try? Of course, there's still some feelings of remorse for you or you would be deceased already. Listen to this last warning, my boy: Do not harm Annania, or your joy ride of life will end. Now go away. I'm busy," responded Frederic as he returned his gaze back to his reading.

As "the Man" reluctantly walked away, he commented almost like an echo, "She will know the truth. You all shall die."

After he was gone, Frederic thought aloud, "Won't ever happen. He knows my limitations. Well, time to call it a night."

The Ending

Finally, the night came; time for some decision making. Sophia and I awaited Frederic in the garden. He was to bring Kelli, so she could make her choice.

But Kelli was lingering in Derrek's room, waiting for him, wondering why he wasn't there. Pondering through some junk on his nightstand she found a small note written to her. Unfolding it she read it aloud…

Dearest Kelli,

Hey sweetheart, I'm so sorry to do this to you, but I have no choice now. I've left for London and will not return for you. I was stupid to believe I could ever marry you. Please do not come looking for me. You will not like what you might find. I can see your family dislikes me, and I know they would never accept us being together. I'd rather be dead if we cannot be together on our own terms. Please understand I will be no more by the time you read this note. Know this, I will never stop loving you and adoring you.

  Derrek

Tears rolling down her warm cheeks, she crumpled the note up dropping it to the floor. Silence. What could be said? He was gone.

Turning toward the door, Frederic was standing in the door. Reaching his arms out as if to console her, she placed her entire being in his cold embrace, sobbing greatly. No words were spoken.

After a few seconds, her sobbing stopped.

Frederic spoke, "It's time to go, my dear. Time to make your decision."

Walking to the garden in dreadful silence, Kelli was in deep thought. At the sight of her mother standing next to me, Kelli bolted straight to her arms hugging her ever so tightly. Unknown to Sophia as to why Kelli was so tearful, she returned the embrace.

"What's upsetting you? Why such sadness?" Sophia pleaded.

"It's Derrek, mother. He's gone. He left me this note telling me he's done with me, with life. I can't believe he just left like that!"

"Wow. Something's not right. I'm sure there's a logical explanation for this…" Sophia responded as she glanced my direction.

"Dry your tears, Kelli. We must get on with this. It ends tonight," I sternly interrupted.

Kelli looked up at me from her mother's embrace and said, "It's your fault. I just know it is. It's always been your fault."

Rolling my eyes in disgust, I thought to myself, *If only I could just bite her…* But instead of that I said, "Enough of this pity. Let's get this over with, so we all can move forward with our eternally damned lives. Frederic, you want to proceed?"

I thought silently to myself as Frederic led Kelli to the little metal bench in the center of the flower garden that maybe this was all my fault. What's done was done now. I knew Kelli loved that boy. She would be fine. She was only hurting right now. She would soon see it was all for the best.

Kneeling beside her, taking hold of her hand ever so gently, Frederic asked, "Kelli, when you are ready tell us your decision."

"Well, I'm definitely ready."

She just sat there staring at us with rage in her eyes, pain in her eyes, not speaking a word.

Sophia broke this silence, anxiously, "Just tell us your choice, Kelli!"

Without anymore hesitation, Kelli spoke these words as she looked at Sophia and I, "Really I would like to destroy you all for the pain and heartache you've put me through recently, especially Annania. But I do love you both, even Frederic, you're all I've ever known. I've no reason to journey this life of mine as a mortal. So, the only choice I can make now is to be immortal. A monstrous being as you are. I choose to be a vampire for all eternity from this moment on."

As soon as she spoke these words, Frederic swiftly sank his teeth into her pale flesh. I'm not quite sure Kelli knew what hit her. Never seeing him in this fashion. He could feel her, see her life as it was, feel her pain and her love for Derrek. It struck hard at his senseless heart.

My thoughts were scrambled as Sophia and I just stood there watching in bewilderment. Sophia had tears forming in her eyes. We had no idea that he would do it in this manner. Had I done the right thing? No time to think this now. Frederic released her. Taking a goblet from beside the bench he lifted her wrist over it, slitting her wrist, emptying her blood into it. Kelli lay there on this damp cold bench, lifeless it seemed. Placing her arm back across her lap, he stood over. Moaning out in a torturous cry, Kelli slowly opened her mouth as to invite his blood in. Frederic leaned closer to her giving her his blood from his wrist. Afterwards, he gave her the blood from the goblet, her own blood. She drank it greedily. When finished, Kelli looked up at us dropping the goblet to the ground.

All three of stood in amazement as we watched Kelli violently start to shake, like in convulsions. Her skin grew paler and her eyes darkened. Sophia was frantic, burying her face in her hands. I was speechless. I hid my face in Frederic's chest. I just couldn't watch this any longer. She seemed so tormented, like being possessed, as she furled among the dirt.

Suddenly, she stopped and laughed out loud as she lay there.

Finally she passed out, oblivious to us. Leaving her laying there, we all decided to return to house. It could take hours before she awoke, who could know.

Sophia lifted the silence as we seated ourselves at the bar in the kitchen.

"Well, I'm glad it's finally over and done. Wonder how long she will be out there like that? And why do I suspect you, Annania, for Derrek's 'disappearance.'"

"You'll know soon enough, Sophia. Now quit badgering me and wait to see what happens next."

At this moment, Frederic stood and said, "I suppose my services are no longer needed. Good bye Sophia, good luck with Kelli and the best of wishes. And to my darling, Annania, I shall see you again soon. Until then, my love, be safe and carry on. I love you, my darling."

After a long, passionate kiss, he left me, just like that. I love that damn vampire so much.

Sophia and I still anxiously waited for Kelli. We sat there making small talk, chatting about nonsense, both avoiding the real issues. It felt like it was hours passing by. I remember a distinct part of our conversation…

"Annania, do you ever wonder if fairies are real? Werewolves? I mean, think about it, they say we do not exist, but here we are."

"Now that's funny. I never thought of it. Well, I can honestly say I've never seen any, but who knows? I had never seen a vampire but look at us now."

"I think it would be so cool to have a pet fairy, or better yet, a pet werewolf. You know, to guard us by day and all that silliness," Sophia said jokingly.

"I'm just fine having my vamp fur babies. They are the only pets I will ever need. That makes me think though, I wonder if there are more like us out there. But truthfully, I'm okay not knowing."

"Yeah, guess you're right. Probably bring more complications to us anyways. It's better to be to ourselves than out there looking for more troubles," Sophia stated with a sly grin.

Finally Kelli graced us with her presence, as she strolled through the door.

"I'm hungry for blood, Mother. Not chicken blood this time. I feel amazing."

"That's nice, dear. Now come with me," I stated

with boldness as I grabbed her arm dragging her behind me.

Sophia was right on our heels as we approached the little cemetery. I knew Kelli was still nasty toward me, but I had to show her what I done.

"Let go of my arm. Where are we going? I need blood," Kelli argued.

"You can have your precious blood in a few moments but first I have to show you something."

So, my conscience was haunting me. I've had enough secrecy. I knew Sophia was suspicious, but she will see. I could feel her eyes pounding at me, no, talking harshly at me, even though she didn't speak.

As we were getting closer to the tomb where I threw his miserable being, we could smell the scent of death all around us. The stench was so strong to our nostrils that we had to cover our noses with our shirt sleeves.

Upon reaching the small stone door of the tomb where Derrek's body lay, I opened it reluctantly. I did not want to experience what was about to behold us.

Kelli shouted about the time I pulled the stone back, "What are you doing? Do you plan to kill us now?"

"No, you idiot. Just shut your mouth, and you'll see. Sophia, please hold on to your daughter as tightly as you can. Thanks."

I knew Sophia knew what might be inside.

As Sophia held Kelli the best she could, I entered the tomb dragging a body out behind me.

Kelli squirmed free of her mother's grip just in time to see who was laying at my feet. It was Derrek. She cussed at me as she dropped beside him.

"He's not dead yet!" Kelli shouted at me.

"I know, silly girl. I saved him for you to decide whether he bleeds to death, or you can just turn him. Your decision. I wanted to kill him completely, but I cared too much for your ass. Sophia, shall we return home?"

Walking back up to the house, I could feel Sophia's anger.

"Did it have to be this way, Annania? I know it was you who wrote that note to Kelli. You should have let her decide on her own instead of pushing her in the direction you wanted. I'm sure she would've made a good choice. Deep down, she does love us."

"Oh, stop Sophia. I'm tired and in need of rest. Hope Kelli decides what to do with him before daybreak. Besides, I told you she would be fine."

Rolling her eyes at me, Sophia said, "What's done can't be undone."

After entering the house, we made our way to our coffin, settled in and slept.

Yes, my dreams came…

Sophia and I were in this dark moist tomb with barely the light of the moon shining through. I could see Derrek laying at our feet. He was dead. With blood on my hands, I knew it was me who murdered him.

Kelli was there shouting at me as she hovered over Derrek's cold lifeless body.

"It's all your fault, Annania!"

Sophia began struggling with her to quiet down but she became more outraged. Suddenly Kelli drove a knife into the side of Sophia's temple. I was raging in anger by now. Before I could attack her, she dropped Sophia's limp body to the dirt floor and shouted at me, "I'm a monster now, and you both shall die!"

As Kelli bolted at me, I saw Sophia turn to ashes. Noticing my legs were slowly fading into a pile of ash, I cried out to Kelli, who was now frozen in her tracks just staring at me.

"Why? Why would you do this to us, Kelli?"

She only laughed a piercing laugh. It echoed loudly in my ears until…

I awoke, shaking terribly as I lay there in my coffin with Sophia next to me. Trying to calm myself, I slowly began running my fingertips through her long hair, thinking, *She's all I have. I will never allow anything or anyone to ever harm her.* Drifting off back to my slumber, I knew I would be fine.

Meanwhile, Kelli was lying beside Derrek in that old tomb as she pondered on what to say to him when he awakes. Her thoughts were, *I have to tell him everything. Maybe not about this curse that I have to bear now. It can wait, or maybe I just won't tell him anything. Oh, I curse you, Annania, for doing this to me.*

After several peaceful, silent moments as she lay there holding him in her embrace, Derrek awoke. Looking around, he wondered where he was, what was happening.

"What's going on? Why am I craving blood? Where are we?" Derrek pleaded.

Kelli chuckled a small laugh and said, "Derrek, you know I love you. And this is going to sound bizarre, but we are in a tomb in this tiny graveyard below our home. You and I are now vampires. I had no other choice but to turn you. You would have died. I know that sounds crazy, but it's true. No, you are definitely not dreaming. Let's get out of her before the sun rises. I will tell you everything that's happened."

Not sure how to take all this in, Derrek stood, following behind Kelli as they ventured out of the tomb and back to the house.

Rushing around before anyone noticed, they quickly began to pack their few belongings. Kelli only stopping long enough to write a small note.

"I think we can make it to London before day break if we hurry. I have a small apartment there. These people, these things, whatever they are seem insane here. And now we are those same creatures! I always knew there was something wrong about your family. This is all mind blowing to me at the moment," Derrek expressed.

Kelli responded as she lay her pen down on the night table, "Sounds good to me. But we need to take that large brown trunk in the corner with us. Looks like we can both fit in it. Don't look at me like that, Derrek. I'm not nuts. The sunlight will hurt us. We will have to sleep in it when we get to where we are going. It will work until we can get something better. The funny thing is, Annania gave me this trunk awhile back, telling me I might need it someday."

"If you say so, sweetheart. Still hard for me to believe I'm immortal. I'll live forever. So surreal," Derrek said as he grinned devilishly.

"Let's go. I'm done here."

On their way out, Kelli slid the note under her mother's door, with eyes shut and her hand placed on the door facing she whispered, "I will never forget you two. Only love remains now."

And so, they begin their journey to London, taking the curse with them.

Awaking the following evening just as the sun was going down, I found the note from Kelli lying on the floor just past the doorway. Yes, I knew she left; I heard her whisper at my door. I probably could have tried to stop her from going, but it would have angered me. No need to kill them both. Picking the note up, I read it aloud to Sophia.

Dearest Mother and Annania,

I never wish to see either of you again. Yes, I do love you both, but I cannot help but blame

you for all of this. Especially you, Annania.
Thanks again for ruining our mortal lives. I
will, in time, forget about this whole painful
experience. One day, I will tell Derrek about
my curse that you placed upon me. We are
going to start a new life in London. Please
stay away from us. Tell Frederic to stay away
as well. We want to be left alone.

Oh, and by the way, I helped myself to
some of your funds. Hope you don't mind!
Trust me, your curse will be safe with me. I
don't know how, but I will carry it on. It shall
be fulfilled so do not worry.

Goodbye.

Kelli

Sophia was speechless, snatching the note from my hands and tearing it into pieces, dropping them to the floor. Seeing tears swell up in her eyes, she just looked at me with a harsh stare.

She spoke, "You did cause all of this. But I'm glad it's over. I miss her already. At least they are immortal now and can fend for their selves. Kelli better be alright. Safe. This curse will devour her if she lets it. I'm gonna be so worried about her. Annania, why must you always do things your way? You should have let her make her decision instead of forcing her into this. Now our own fates rest in Kelli's hands. And no communication with her could be bad. Who knows what will become of us all now? I need blood, lots of it. Let's go, shall we?"

Following her, I was somewhat shocked at her words to me, her mere tone. I had never really heard her speak to me in this way, but who could blame her. I would be disgusted at myself too. Kelli was her child. But, it was done, and I have no regrets on how it all went down. The hurt and hard feelings will be forgotten in time. Because that's all we have is time and each other.

Strolling the dark streets of Paris, I spoke after several steps of silence.

"Kelli will be okay. She's strong and you know it. Who knows, she might return to us someday when fear of this curse hits her. I can almost feel it. She will be back. I'm almost sure of it. And when she does, we can help her then. I'm not really caring if Derrek survives or not though. Guess we shall see in time."

Sophia just stooped walking and hugged me tightly. It scared me a little.

"It's over, Annania. It's just us now. Let's do it like we used to in the early years. You take one, and I take the other. I need some fun. And in a few nights, we can watch for the news to report the murders. Shall we go?"

"Ah, my sweet Sophia! You never hold a grudge very long."

After several nights of feasting on estranged victims, Sophia and I decided to spend this night in our flower garden. Relaxing, talking, trying to avoid the past experiences from the last few nights. Talking of endless nonsense, we heard a strange noise coming from behind us like an animal moving about in the bushes.

Turning, we saw "the Man" standing right behind us. I was frozen in my seat with fear, but Sophia speedily reacted, jumping to her feet away from him, and shouted, "Kill him before he kills us!"

Startled, I reacted by placing myself in front of Sophia, not letting her attack this fiend. Fearfully, I noticed his eyes.

"Sophia, calm yourself. I don't think he's going to hurt us this night."

She looked at me in mere amazement.

Coming just slightly closer to us, "the Man" seated himself on the grass in front of us. He gestured for us to the same. Hesitantly, I pulled at Sophia to seat herself with me. After we were seated, he spoke, "I must tell you, Annania, what happened to me. My story. Please do not speak a word until I'm finished. No worries. I will not harm you tonight."

Sitting there not able to speak, we both were afraid but curious.

He continued, "As you know, I cared for Frederic, staying with him for a long time in Ireland after he found me as a lad. I was never really aware of what happened to my family. You see, Frederic became like a father to me. He gave me all I could ever dream of, all I could ever desire. He showed me love beyond my comprehensive knowledge. But it all ended. The very night while he was at his desk in the study, I asked him about my parents' death. I needed to know what had become of them. He truthfully told me that he was the one who had taken their blood, killing them. I was to be next, but he fell in love with me the moment he laid eyes on me as I lay sleeping. He had to keep me for his own. I had no memory of him ever being in my parents' house.

When I woke up that night, so long ago, I was in a bed with pure silk sheets. The room was huge and dark. I was afraid. I was only a teenager. He had taken me from my home to his castle in Ireland. He never spoke of what really happened to my parents until I asked him that night. He had always avoided my questions, never answering them. So, as time went by, I belonged to him. Anyway, that same night, I became angered, enraged at him. How could he take me way from my loved ones like that? Whether you believe me or not, Annania, he murdered your family as well. This evil being called Frederic cannot be alone. He has to have his companion, control over someone. The night you met him, he was only there for you from the start. He wanted you, same as he wanted me back then. I was surprised he spared your dear Sophia."

Boldly interrupting him, I declared, "No, you lie! Frederic loves me. He only does what's necessary for our love to be strong. He would never do anything to hurt me or Sophia! I cannot believe these things you say!"

Calming myself, with Sophia caressing my hand, I settled down enough to hear the rest of his story.

Smiling at me, Samuel continued, "I was angry at Frederic for days; we argued constantly. Hatred started setting in the more I was near him. Nearing my twenty-first birthday, I wanted my freedom. To be on my own. I had to get away from him. Of course, all this time, I knew his little immortal secret. One early evening just past sun down, I had enough of it. I went to his room, pulling him from his coffin. It definitely infuriated him. He shouted at me very loudly. He told me I was never to disturb him while he slept. I really wanted to destroy him—everything about him. He had ruined my life. Never any chances of having a normal existence now. You see, I failed to mention that he tried on several occasions to turn me. I always refused his offers.

"I had already met and fell in love with a beautiful lady in the town village, but Frederic killed her immediately after finding out. Pure Jealousy. You will know, Annania, soon enough how jealous of a vampire he really is. Anyway, back to the evening I disturbed him. I was prepared for a fight if it needed to be. I tried to attack him after he shouted at me, driving my dagger into his chest. But no avail. He could not die. I knew this.

But I so longed to be free of him. He was a killer, an awful being, evil. And he wanted to make me into one of these. Frederic pulled the knife from his chest laughing dropping it to the floor. Afraid, I stumbled over my own feet. He came at me slinging me around the room several times, until finally he attacked me, burying his fangs into my neck.

"I passed out, only to awaken several nights later. Frederic was gone, along with all his belongings. I searched for what seemed like centuries but never found him. You see, this is why I have the scars on my face. I woke that night to find I was all cut up. I had a strange taste in my mouth like blood but I didn't know why. I've lived a long time in between humanity and the undead, but I have never stolen someone's blood from them. I'm really not sure what keeps me alive, unless it's blood from Frederic. This devil of a man defeats every time I attempt to destroy him. But I vowed to myself that I will never give up. I will end his immortal life one day. He will die, miserably.

"Annania, I hope you can comprehend all this, and see why I hate him so much. I know you've already seen some of my pain the night you assaulted me. I must go now, but I will be watching. Someday your time will come, but not this night. I will end all of Frederic's creations."

He stood swiftly, leaning over me and kissing my forehead, and just like that he was gone, disappeared.

Still in a state of shock, I asked Sophia, "What are you thinking?"

"I'm not sure exactly what to think. Frederic, controlling? Hard to believe. Aside from being afraid, I felt sorry for that guy. So much hatred inside him. It's quite sad."

"Well, I've no doubt my Frederic loves me. Not that interested in what happened between him and Samuel. Oh, by the way that's his name. Frederic and I had a vague discussion about 'the Man' some time ago. I feel a slight remorse for Samuel, but we still need to be cautious of him. I find it impossible to believe my beloved Frederic could take my parents in that manner, especially since I know how much he cares for me, for us. He wouldn't let anything hurt us, Sophia."

Giggling slightly, Sophia said, "Well, there's no guessing, but that guy's life went terribly wrong. His story was very disturbing. You bet we will be cautious of this Samuel."

As we prepared for our sweet slumber, I waited for Sophia to drift off to sleep. Thinking to myself of how much I was in love with Frederic, my heart ached for Samuel. So much pain and hatred toward our kind. If his story were true, he suffered through a lot. But I just couldn't find it in myself to believe my beloved Frederic could be so evil. I thought it best to never bring this up to Frederic; it would only anger him. Besides, how could I know what was the truth? I slowly drifted into a deep sleep.

My dreams occurred again…

Out of curiosity I eased over to Frederic and "the Man" as they were discussing me. There seemed to be a debate between them. As I approached, Frederic greeted me softly saying, "My darling, you must decide. You have to choose between us. You know all too well that I will never allow any harm to come to you."

"No. Annania you have to believe me. He's dangerous and evil. You can live a better life with me knowing you'll never harm anyone else. Or I can end it all now for you," Samuel stated boldly.

Frightened at such boldness from them both, I shouted "No!" as I tried to back away. "What is this madness you speak of? How can I make a choice like this? You're both scaring me!"

Right before my eyes, Samuel pulled his dagger, slicing my Frederic's throat, his lifeless body crumpling to the ground. Screaming to the point of my voice going hoarse as my tears flowed down my face, I accused, "You're a monster! Why kill my love?"

As he disappeared into the misty fog of the night, he chanted at me, "It's all your fault!"

He was gone. I was alone. Frederic's body evaporated into ashes.

I awoke breathing uncontrollably, feeling afraid, thinking to myself, *Will "the Man" destroy us all? How? When?*

Calming my nerves, I thought about how all these night terrors were starting to affect me. It seemed I

couldn't think straight afterwards. There was such torment inside me lately.

Shaking these thoughts from my mind, I finally
calmed myself and snuggled in to Sophia, who lay
peaceably next to me falling asleep.

Still haunted by Samuel's appearance, I sat alone in
the garden, one seemingly peaceful evening dwelling
on my own dreadful thoughts. Gazing up at the clear
starry night, I pondered over in my head all the things
that has happened recently. Trying my best to justify it
all, I found myself coming back to all the words "the
Man" said to us.

Feeling self-pity, almost useless, for all eternity, I
must only kill to survive. How can I abide in such
misery? Haunting my dreams, I am a killer, and my
eternal torment will be my loved ones being destroyed. Confusing my own thoughts, how could I
ever leave Sophia? What of my love? I could never
choose between her or Frederic. It would be a vast
void in my world without them both, such emptiness
it would cause. My love for them is strong, endless. I
may be a soulless fiend, but I still care. My beloved
Frederic only needs to be loved, cared for. Sophia
needs me also. I have to figure a way to love them
separately. He knows I will never part from her, of
that I am sure.

Interrupting my pathetic mood swing, Sophia
strolled up next to me seating herself beside me.

"Don't speak yet," I mumbled. "Let me finish lingering in my darkness alone. No fear of what will be now. I just want to continue feeling sorry for myself while I dwell in my own miserable wicked thoughts. I know what you might be wondering, Sophia. You want to know what will become of us now it's all over, am I right?"

"Yes, you're right. I do think of it, but it's over and done. Can't change it. I hope Kelli is wise and makes the right choices. Don't be too long out here. Sunrise will come soon. I'll leave you to your self-pity now. Good evening," Sophia stated as she patted my hand, kissing my forehead leaving me to my selfishness.

Smiling, I spoke as she walked away. "Promise, I won't be much longer. I can't let you sleep alone. I'll be right behind you."

After she was gone into the house, my thoughts took me back to my Frederic. Missing him greatly this night, wanting him naughtily, I could almost taste his blood on my lips. I know deep within me, our love will never die. Maybe soon he could stay with me longer instead of always leaving for long periods. Until then, I would await his return eagerly.

Glancing up at the night once more, I whispered to myself, "I will never leave Sophia, no matter how much my Frederic pleads for me to do so. She means too much to me. I'd kill over her. Frederic, you are my love, but Sophia is my eternal companion."

Silently, I had one last thought: *My heart aches at times for Sophia. Especially when I think of all I've done to her. It is my fault we are what we are now. And to think of Kelli, what will become of her? Will she carry this curse, or let us all be no more?*

Sunrise was starting to show signs of coming, so I decided it best to cease these weary thoughts and retire to our coffin, where I was positive Sophia was already resting. Our eternal destiny. Enough pity for this night.

Standing, I blew a kiss to the night sky, whispering aloud, "Goodnight, my love, my Frederic, wherever you may be tonight. Until I see you again."

Entering the doorway, as I scurried up the winding staircase, Samuel met me unexpectedly at the top step. All I could do was gaze into his hollow eyes as he stared at me. Feeling his arm slip around my waist as he pulled me close to him, I felt hypnotized unable to move. There was no love in his eyes, only hate. His lips were cold as they touched mine.

Smelling Frederic's scent of blood on his lips I froze inside as my fangs contracted. Angered and afraid, my mind was in a whirlwind. Smelling the scent of death all around him. What had he done? Why? Impulsively coming to my senses, I pushed away from him struggling to be free of his strong embrace.

"Let me go!" I pleaded. "What have you done? Where is Frederic?"

Laughing slightly at me, he devilishly responded, "Your beloved Frederic will soon be no more. You are so blinded by what is the truth."

"No! You're lying to me!" I shouted as I ran from him to my room slamming my door behind me.

As I leaned against the door, breathing in a slight panic, I slowly turned around opening the door peeking out to see if he was still out there. No one. I tried to sense his presence but to no avail. I whispered to myself, "Where is he? Will he really hurt my Frederic?"

Closing the door tightly, I locked it as I thought about the scent of Frederic's blood on his lips. It seemed so fresh. Surely "the Man" can't destroy him. He doesn't seem to be strong enough. Taking in a few deep, calming breaths, I slowly made my way to my coffin, laying myself next to Sophia who was sleeping soundly. I slept.

The next evening after awakening, I was at my desk thinking of Frederic and how it would be nice to see him this night. Hoping he would come to me. Entering the room, Sophia stepped into the closet.

"Where are you going tonight? You know you can't stay here. He may come at any time. I can't help but feel he's coming to me," I said teasingly to her.

"Don't worry. I'll be gone. In fact, I'm leaving now. I only needed a thin jacket to complete my outfit. Not sure what I'm going to do tonight. Was thinking about going to the far side of town, the gutters, and see what kind of trash I can find to feed on. Feeling a little wicked tonight. Besides I've never hunted in that area. Could be fun. Maybe I can get lucky and find me a handsome vampire to fall madly in love with while I'm out," Sophia playfully stated.

As she left, I found myself daydreaming, or should I say night dreaming, as I peered through the curtain of my window, focusing at the well-lit moon. Hearing a slight noise in the hedges below, I saw what looked like a shadow of a man moving about in the moonlight. I thought, *It can't be Frederic. I do not smell his scent. Could it be Samuel back again? Why must he always watch us?*

Before I could investigate any further, someone touched my shoulder. I jumped in fear, only to see my beloved Frederic laughing at me.

"You scared me!" I hissed at him as I threw myself into his arms, kissing his lips as hard as I could. Holding me closer, he caressed my body as we held this ever so passionate kiss. Like lovers who hadn't seen each other for years.

Sinking my fangs into his vein, I could taste his warm blood, so satisfying. As we slowly fell to the floor in a tight embrace, I allowed him to taste me, to get his fill. Completely giving myself to his lust. I honestly forgot about the shadow outside. I was in total ecstasy. The world did not exist around me.

Afterward, we lay in each other's embrace, as he kissed me with blood stained lips. Staying here for what seemed like hours holding each other, we talked non-sense, and finally he told me more of his place in Paris.

"Annania, you must come with me tonight. Your friend can take care of herself. You deserve my love and for me to care for you. Only I can make you feel this every night. This fantasy. My mansion is beautiful, filled with only the finest furniture you could ever hope for. Many horses are free to roam with land beyond what the eye can see. You even have your very own cof-fin right beside mine in a secure, fully furnished bed-room suite. It's made of pure clear glass, so I can always gaze upon you while I lay next to you. Annania, you have to see it. We can always be together, never apart anymore. You'll have the full control of the home, and I can always keep a better watch on you."

"Oh, my Frederic, I would love to be with you in-definitely. To wake up next to you each evening, it would be such fantasy, amazing. But you know already that I cannot leave Sophia. She needs me. Besides, what if Kelli shall return, and I'm not here to help?"

"It seems to me, Annania, that Sophia could help Kelli herself. She is her mother after all. I seriously doubt that will happen though. Kelli is long gone with that wretched love of hers," Frederic stated boldly.

"Please, let's not talk of this anymore tonight," I begged. "Let's just enjoy each other some more this night. I would like to hear more about your travels. I really enjoy your stories, my love."

As he went on and on about his travels, his journeys I peacefully listened until I was so hypnotized by his mere voice, I faded into a deep relentless slumber, fully relaxed in his embrace.

Meanwhile, Sophia had started her own little adventure. Killing several homeless humans on her way to the gutters across down, she was feeling fearless. Like she was unstoppable.

Seeing a lady out of the corner of her eye up in the distance, Sophia could sense this was not a human. She was tall and lean, had beautiful figure. Like a dancer concentrating on her every move. Gracefully, this woman was like a statue of beauty. Her hair was fiery red with skin like a milky-white being. Her green-hazel eyes were dazzling. Wonderfully beautiful, this creature was to look upon. She seemed to float across the cobblestone street. Now she was so close to Sophia you could actually feel her breath in front of you. Nervously, Sophia just stared into her eyes, when she spoke these words…

"You must be one of Frederic's. I see he's been busy since making me."

"No," Sophia quickly corrected. "I'm of someone else creation."

"But you smell of Frederic's blood."

"Well, the one who made me was made by him," responded Sophia.

"I see. Have you heard then of the horrid curse upon our gender?"

"Of course I have, I'm the one who had to bear it. I've already gave birth to a girl child to save our kind. I thought we were the only female vampires created. Who are you?" Sophia answered her sharply.

Laughing a small chuckle, she said, "I'm Lucille. I have some knowledge to enrich you with. Shall we walk and chat together?"

Sophia was full of curiosity. Who was this vampire? How did she know Frederic?

As they strolled together, Lucille had a crooked smile on her face as she began to tell her story...

"I'm Frederic's first. There may be more made from him, but I cannot be sure. His quest for an eternal lover to control has tormented him for centuries. I, too, was told of the curse, and I bore a child, a boy child."

"Was he a monster?" Sophia shockingly interrupted.

"That's what I was going to say. No, he wasn't. In time, I found out that he's made a lot of women vampires after me, and their male children were not savages. Frederic is a controlling fiend after he lures you in. He wants full control of whomever he makes. I feel his philosophy of this so-called curse is at an end, like a dying breed. Many of the other vampires who still believe in the old customs that women should not be vampires are becoming extinct."

"What do you mean 'old customs'? About our gender?" Sophia questioned.

"I mean, the ones who believe in the old ways. Who think women shouldn't be vampires. They were strict on the belief that if a male vampire makes a female into a vampire, he should control her, like ownership. But it never really worked for me after Frederic changed me. He couldn't keep me, control me. I think he tells his ladies that it is forbidden to make a female vampire. Frederic may seem nice and a gentleman, but he's evil, selfishly so. He took my only son from me and locked me away to die in a glass coffin. His plan was to let the sun rise over my coffin. It was a terrible experience. I will never forget it. The ceiling of this huge room opened up, just split apart, right as the sun was peeking out. But before it could burn me further, I was saved. Some vampires I knew had rescued me. We torched the house and fled from there. I still live with these friends. I've searched for years for my son, but to no avail. I just can't accept the fact that he's dead. I feel he cannot die with Frederic's blood flowing within him. He wasn't a monster. He was a beautiful boy, normal it seemed. His name was Samuel. You and your friend should flee from this devil of a vampire the first chance you get. I hope his evil will be destroyed."

Standing there in shock, Sophia only blinked, and this woman was gone as fast as she came. Feeling the rain starting to fall as it hit her face, she quietly made her way back to home. The rain was getting harder as Sophia thought of all Lucille had told her. Talking to herself she said, "Should I tell all of this to Annania? Would she even believe me? Where was this Lucille from? Where did she go?"

Deciding to herself, Sophia figured it best to keep quiet for a while on this. Besides, she knew I was too headstrong to fall for anything Frederic had up his sleeve. And there's no way I would ever have a child as long as I was with Frederic.

So, he must really love her. Either way my eyes will definitely be watching him, Sophia decided within her thoughts.

Arriving home with all this still on her mind, Sophia was quiet with a faraway stare, barely speaking a word to me. I knew something had to be bothering her, but thought maybe she'd talk about it when she was ready. I even wondered why she was blocking me from her mind. It must have been something really important that she wasn't not ready to talk about. Oh well, she would tell me in time.

As we lay in our eternal bed, I could sense Sophia was still battling something in her thoughts. Deciding not to press the matter, I snuggled in close to her as we fell into a deep slumber.

As I slept, I only thought of Frederic, wishing he could have stayed with me. During this relaxed state of sleep I was in, my dreams began to flash in my mind.

Seeing myself as a small girl laying in my mother's bed, I saw a hooded, horrible creature hovered over me holding a crooked ax in his hand. He looked to be my death. I had heard stories from my father about the Grim Reaper, but I never believed them. While I was thinking this, I started to cry for help, but no one noticed. This thing grabbed me lifting me up while it raised its ax as if to swing it at me. Just as the ax pierced my throat I awoke.

Awake and nervous while I lay next to Sophia, I noticed there was a pale light shining in through a crack in our coffin. Someone had tried to raise the lid. Easing the lid up I saw sunlight beaming around the room. Burning my eyes, the sun was fierce. I could barely see, but "the Man" was standing right over us. His dagger was raised and coming straight down toward my neck.

So, he's finally destroying us, I thought to myself, just like he kept promising to do.

Missing me, his dagger went straight into Sophia's chest. Screaming at him while my flesh burned from the sunlight, I begged him to stop, but I was paralyzed. I couldn't move no matter how hard I tried. Sophia's body was turning to ashes by the sun. My legs were starting to become ash as well. "The Man" was nowhere in sight now. I pleaded for help, but no such luck, when I heard his faint chanting… "It's all your fault. And now you will die."

I tried to move, but my legs were nothing but ash. I was helpless. Yelling louder for help, still no one came. Suddenly, I saw Samuel standing over me as struggled to move. His knife was coming right for my chest. Looking in his dark hollow eyes full of hatred, I felt the blade pierced my chest...

I awoke. Silence.

The only sound was my heavy breathing. Blood sweat dripping off my brows. Doing my best to calm down, I gently curled back up to Sophia after scanning my coffin for any light. Drifting back off into a finally restful sleep, all I could do was think, *This dream seems by far the worst and it stayed with me for quite a few nights.* The most frightening part of this dream was I knew not when or how Samuel would try to kill us. We got to stay more cautious of him.

Some nights later...

I was still having my nightmares, these horrible dreams, but still I failed to mention anything about them to Sophia, and especially to Frederic. As I've said before, this was my eternal torment due to the horrifying fiend I am. Sophia still wasn't acting like herself lately. I knew she was keeping something from me, but what could I do. She got aggravated at me if I only mentioned what's on her mind.

As I sit here writing this book, a dream comes to mind that I had forgotten, knowing it could never be so...

In this dream, I'm dead. Laying in a pearl white coffin. It's my funeral. Everyone is standing in the daytime rain, crying around me. As I lay in this open, wet coffin, I notice I'm wearing a beautiful, elegant wedding dress, so white and bright. Blood red roses are all around me. I look so peaceful as I lay there lifeless and cold, wet. My lid is closed, and now I'm being lowered into the ground. Dirt is being thrown on top of my coffin. Everyone is dropping a single blood red rose onto my grave as I see them walk away, crying.

Suddenly, everyone is laughing at me, as the rain is falling harder and harder. They are screaming now, "It's all your fault!" They say these words loudly over and over until it maddens me as I lay in my death bed. Tossing and turning in this coffin, I try to free myself as I cry out that I'm not really dead. No one can hear my pleading. They only laughed louder.

Then, I awake to find I'm still here. Still a monstrosity, still a horrible fiend, and will be throughout eternity.

In my human days, there was a Bible verse that always calmed my fear. And now from time to time, Frederic will quote it to me in his French accent…

Car Dieu a tant aime lemonde qu'll a donne son
Fils unique, a fin que quiconque croit
Enluine perisse point, mais qu'll ait lavie eternelle.

(John 3:16)

"For God so loved the world that He gave his only begotten Son, that whosoever believeth in Him should not perish but have everlasting life"(John 3:16). Strange really, why this would still comfort me. Don't you think?

On this night, I still awoke before Sophia. Letting her sleep, I decided to break from writing and take a walk. Going further than I normally do, I came up on a dreary hollow of wilted grass and trees. With the foggy mist settling over the tall pines reminded me of a weeping willow. The night was so peaceful, lovely, almost ghastly. Sitting by myself what seemed like hours, I wondered, *Why did it have to come to this?*

Slipping off the damp tree stump, I walked on through the hollow trees with my arms outstretched, almost floating. Wishing God would end this life of mine as this evil creature I've become. I thought again, *Why, Frederic, did you make what I am?*

Settling in underneath a wet, cold tree, branches hovered over me. I closed my eyes, trying to imagine that I did not exist. So much has happened in this wretched thing I call a life. Overwhelming me, I thought how I couldn't even call any of this a lifetime. My life will never end. This must be my eternal damnation, these depressing thoughts. My guilt tries to overtake me as I think of all those miserable souls I massacred, yet the wickedness inside me enjoys it.

Coming back to my reality, I gradually made my way back toward home, where I was to live with my Sophia forever in our nasty yet wonderful life, if you can call this living. Dwelling in my pain, I saw a face in the fog ahead of me. It was a girl; no, wait, a young woman, maybe in her twenties. She was holding a new-born baby, smelling of fresh blood. Such a hunger rose in my undead body. Racing to her side, I took her before she even knew I was there—

Just playing, I stopped myself and decided to hunt on.

As I passed by her and the baby, I read her thoughts. She was an outsider, tossed out because she couldn't withhold from the sins of the flesh. Deciding I was going to help them, I swiftly picked them up returning home to Sophia. Of course, she was frightened beyond belief, but it would be alright. She made no attempts to free herself. Sophia and I cleaned them up and gave the woman a large sum of money to live comfortably for a very long while. The woman never spoke but nodded to us gratefully. You could tell she was still fearful of us but never acted on it. We found her a nice flat above the little café, making the owner promise to keep an eye on her and the baby, or it would end badly for him with his precious life.

While kissing them both goodbye, she finally spoke. She wanted to know our names. Leaning into her I whispered ever so gently in her ear, "We're your guardian angels in disguise."

Sophia was loving the little baby boy as she made promises to the mother that she'd visit as often as possible. Leaving them to their short human lives, I began thinking of how extraordinary it would be to start a new life, start over fresh and new. Relive one's life. Would I make similar choices again? Would I choose this lifestyle all over again? Would I do it again to Sophia? Make her suffer through it all again?

Breaking my thoughts, Sophia asked, "A penny for your thoughts?"

"Oh, my thoughts? How about yours lately?"

Sophia gave me a sinister stare.

"Nevermind!" I responded promptly. "I was just pondering in my brain what it would be like to start over, our lives fresh and new. Do you really feel like that woman and her baby is going to make it in this world? A cast away with no man to father her baby. Hope she can support that baby on what cash we gave her."

"Start over? Why would we want to do that? Either way, we will always be side by side. Good or bad, it will always be us no matter what choices was made. And yes, I think those two will be just fine. We will make sure of that. I'm pretty damn sure that mother will raise that baby boy to be a fine gentleman."

"But, Sophia, wouldn't you like to be human again, feel the sunshine on your face and seeing things in the day again?"

"Oh please, Annania. Give me some peace and stop with your whining. I can't even remember what I felt like as a human being. Besides the point, I'm hungry.

And it will be daylight soon. Shall we find us a little snack?"

Grinning wickedly, I followed in behind her footsteps as we searched for our first kill of the night.

Assuming this little good deed we did can justify slightly for our souls, if we even have one, once in a while, it helps the conscious mind of a fiend to do a good deed for others, but not too often. We are monstrous by nature, I suppose.

As far as the others go... We haven't heard from Kelli and Derrek, but we can sense their presence at times. I believe they may still abide in London. Sophia and I will pretty much dwell in Paris other than visiting different places from time to time. Frederic still pops in on me on occasion. He will always be the love of my undead life, no matter how much Sophia seems to dislike him. Our Frankie died in Venice, leaving her daughter Angela in charge of our assets. So far, she does a decent job of handling our finances and affairs. We finally broke down and sold our land and little cottage back in Alabama. Who could ever really say if we will return there?

We still feel "the Man" from time to time, but there has been no visual of him lately. Knowing he still watches us, I wonder why he hasn't tried to kill us yet. I'm not sure. I like to think my Frederic has something to do with that, keeping us safe. Of course, I still have my depressed moments within my thoughts. Especially when I think about how I wronged Sophia and put that awful curse on her, and now passed it on to Kelli. But I did it, and it's in the past. Just got to keep moving forward in this eternity. Whether any of it was right or wrong, I'm still tormented in my dreams. Sophia still has times when she seems distant from me, but only in short intervals. I may never know what haunts her.

And so you see most of my story. I will leave you now. I have a knock at my door, an unexpected visitor...

*

Opening my door, I see flowers outside. Black roses with a card that reads as follows...

> *Please know, the curse of a lady vampire shall continue, or will it? I'm back for you, my love.*
>
> *Samuel*

The End

(Perhaps...)